BATTLE *for* LIFE

Scott I. Zucker

authorHOUSE®

AuthorHouse™
1663 Liberty Drive
Bloomington, IN 47403
www.authorhouse.com
Phone: 833-262-8899

Published by AuthorHouse 01/13/2023

ISBN: 978-1-6655-7929-2 (sc)
ISBN: 978-1-6655-7930-8 (e)

Library of Congress Control Number: 2022924018

Print information available on the last page.

Any people depicted in stock imagery provided by Getty Images are models, and such images are being used for illustrative purposes only. Certain stock imagery © Getty Images.

This book is printed on acid-free paper.

This book is dedicated to my dad...and to my sons....and to their children.

Life can be a battle, but worth the fight.

Writer's note

THIS STORY WAS inspired by my father's real-life experience during World War II on the aircraft carrier the USS Bunker Hill, but it is not a story about my father. It is a story about fathers and sons and the connections they share, some spoken and some unspoken. Ultimately, it is a story about loss and love and the battles that each of us face as we go through life.

Acknowledgements

WRITING IS A process that requires both internal and external inspiration. I want to thank my family and friends who have constantly encouraged me to write and, especially on this project, took the time to review my drafts and help guide me towards completion. Much love and thanks to Kevin, Richard, Ken, Jeff and David. But always and most of all, my love and appreciation to Melanie, who knows where these stories come from and understands my need to share them.

Chapter 1

T HE EYELIDS OF his old, tired eyes shifted as his dream became more vivid, and he grew more agitated with the stress of being witness again to the horror that had plagued his dreams for years.

In his fifties and sixties, he had drowned these dreams with bourbon and sleeping pills. But now that he was ninety, his doctor had warned him about the repercussions of mixing too much alcohol with his diabetes and high blood pressure medicines. He wasn't trying to kill himself. He just didn't want to keep reliving the events he knew had changed him forever.

He had received the invitation in the mail. This year, there would be a reunion for the crew of the USS Bunker Hill aircraft carrier on the anniversary of their most famous day of battle during World War II. The Navy recognized the date every ten years through different ceremonies scheduled around the country. He had missed every previous event, thinking there was no reason to congregate over the memory of a fateful experience. But it had now been seventy years, and this would likely be his last chance to acknowledge the anniversary. He was certain that only a handful of men would still be left. But this year, they would gather at the World War II Memorial in Washington, DC, a monument Max had not yet visited. He was curious about the reunion. He had kept the invitation by his bed. It was the invitation that had triggered the recurrence of the dreams.

Chapter 2

THE BUNKER HILL had initially launched on December 7, 1942, exactly one year after the devastation and tragedy at Pearl Harbor. The naval ship was an "Essex Class" aircraft carrier, a massive vessel more than 800 feet long and 100 feet high and weighing over 36,000 tons. The carrier held more than 2,600 men and more than 100 planes above and below deck. It was a floating city.

By the end of 1944, the ship had already seen its share of the war in the Pacific theater. The ship had participated in air raids and flight support for amphibious landings of US troops in the Marshall and Marianas Islands. During those landings in the Marianas, the Bunker Hill suffered its first casualties when a Japanese aerial bomb scattered shrapnel across the sides and deck of the ship. Two sailors were killed, and another eighty were wounded. Notwithstanding heavy fire from Japanese warplanes, the Bunker Hill stood its ground, and its anti-aircraft fire brought down multiple planes. Even damaged, the Bunker Hill then fought in the Battle of the Philippine Sea and supported additional air raids on the Japanese Islands.

In November 1944, the ship returned to the Puget Sound Naval Yard in Bremerton, Washington, for repairs and a weapons upgrade. The ship dry-docked on November 6, 1944 and would remain there until late January 1945. New sailors would join its crew during its holdover. One of them was Max Silver. He was nineteen years old, a seaman first class.

Chapter 3

"**D**AD," SAM CALLED out as he opened the house's side door. That door was never locked, and Sam always wondered how it was possible that no one had ever even tried to rob the place. "Dad," he called out again. It was Sunday, already after 10:00 in the morning. He was sure his dad was awake. He'd always been an early riser.

Sam carried the bag of fresh cold cuts, cream cheese, and bagels into the outdated kitchen and laid the white-wrapped packages of deli meats on the kitchen counter. The Sunday morning delivery had become a weekly tradition for Sam and his dad since Sam's mom had passed away five years before. Sam knew that none of the food was good for his dad, but his dad was always so happy to have the visit and the food, so Sam didn't want to change the routine.

Sam pulled a warm bagel from the bag, ready to start building himself a sandwich, when his dad replied. "I'm in my office," Sam heard his father call out as he began to cut the bagel in half.

Sam left the sliced bagel on the table and walked down the hallway, past the antique-laden living room, into his dad's small office. There were papers everywhere and several empty boxes on the floor. "Dad," he exhaled, looking around. "You're moving in less than a month. I thought you had made some progress in going through this room!"

"I will. I will," his father replied, "but I wanted to show you something first."

Sam thought his dad looked a little disoriented. "What, Dad?

What did you want to show me?" he said, feeling a little exasperated and still thinking about the bagel and cold cuts waiting for him in the other room.

"I wanted to show you this," his dad said, his voice softening as he spoke. Max pulled a pile of black and white photographs from his desk.

Instantly, Sam recognized the group of pictures. They were of assorted sizes, many of them yellowed around their edges. "Dad," he said, "These are amazing. I'm so glad you have these to look back on."

"Seventy years," his dad replied. "Seventy years."

Sam perused the assorted pictures of his father in his dress whites, group pictures with his Navy buddies, and photos of the crew, hundreds and hundreds of men, in perfect formation, spelling out the words "Bunker Hill" on the deck of the carrier.

"It's been seventy years," his dad said again.

Sam couldn't even contemplate what those seventy years meant when his dad referenced the time. Sam was sixty, so the war was already a decade past by the time he was born. And in those seventy years since the end of the war, his father had gotten married, started a business, raised two adult children, and enjoyed two grandchildren. It was a bounty of time that seemed like forever but flashed by instantly.

It was then that his dad handed him the invitation. It read: "Seventieth Reunion of the USS Bunker Hill. World War II Monument, Washington DC."

The event was scheduled for Saturday, May eleventh, less than two weeks away. Sam scanned the invitation and then handed it back to his father.

"I'm going," his father said.

"Really?" Sam asked. In part, he was just trying to grasp the logistics of his elderly father getting anywhere, let alone to Washington, DC.

The embossed invitation was from the US Department of the Navy. It read, "In recognition and celebration of the sailors from the

USS Bunker Hill and their contribution and sacrifice to end World War II."

"Dad." Sam was still trying to organize his thoughts. "This is in less than two weeks. It's probably too late to RSVP. Plus, we have to finish packing you up. You move into the senior living center on June first."

"I want to go," his father said.

"To Washington? Now? Why?" Sam's questions showed his confusion.

His father looked up and then picked up one of the faded black-and-white pictures of the Bunker Hill. "It's been seventy years," he said. "It's time for me to let it go."

Sam didn't want to argue. He had come over because they had a lot of work to do packing up the house so that his father could move. He figured he'd return to the reunion discussion after packing up one of the bedrooms. "How about a bagel, Dad?"

Chapter 4

BEFORE THE WAR, Max had never left New York City. Maybe a few trips to Long Island but nothing like this. Since he enlisted, he had already taken a bus to Florida for basic training and then the transport plane to Washington state. Two hundred men sat in the plane. They were lined up in rows of ten each, dressed in full gear. Each time they hit turbulence, some men around him would vomit, but Max found the flight exhilarating. He was amazed that the plane could stay that long in the sky.

Buses were waiting at the Bremerton airport. The men moved in unison from the plane to the buses. The ride to the naval yard was short but scenic. Max was mesmerized by the views of the mountains that surrounded the city. As they arrived, the newly minted sailors were directed to their assigned ships. Max had no idea he would be sent to work on an aircraft carrier. As he walked with the other new crewmembers toward the carrier, he was overwhelmed by its size and shape. It was the largest ship he had ever seen.

After being assigned his bunk, he was ordered to report to the flight deck to be placed in a working group. Each working group was directed to perform certain repairs on the ship while it was dry-docked. The group would make the repairs during one shift, train for their regular duties during their second shift, and sleep during their third shift.

Max had been designated to the carrier to be a radar man. He showed an aptitude for mathematics and could study the radar screen and plot the movements of ships and planes that appeared on the digital map. Radar interception remained a relatively new phenomenon in the war. Max was proud to be one of the first to use the new equipment. He understood the responsibility of trying to forewarn the ship of impending aerial or submarine attacks. The better they were prepared, the stronger they could be to fight off the attacks. Max would soon learn how vital these skills were.

Max's working group was ordered to install new steel armor plates around the pilot house, which was part of the ship's Command Tower. The metalwork and riveting would take the men at least two weeks to install.

As each man reported to the assigned group, they saluted the ranking lieutenant. One of the first men Max met was Tony Carletto. Tony had transferred to the Bunker Hill after an assignment as a gunner's mate on the USS Massachusetts. The Massachusetts had been part of the same task force as the Bunker Hill in the Marshall Islands. Tony had already served in the Pacific for over a year.

The lieutenant explained to the group of six men that they would do their welding work in two four-hour shifts with a break in the middle. Between shifts, if they weren't in the mess hall getting coffee, they all gathered outside on the ship's rail, smoking. It killed the monotony.

During one of the first breaks, as the men crowded along the deck, Tony reached into his pocket and pulled out a letter he had received, waving it to show to his friends. The letter smelled of perfume. "From home," he said.

"'Dear John' letter?" called out Ryan, one of the guys in the crew.

"Nope." Tony retorted. "She would never give this up!" He gestured to show off his biceps to the other men, who laughed and whistled. Tony was from New Jersey. He prided himself in his Italian heritage, and his slicked-back hair showed off his ever-present confidence and swagger.

Max took a draw from his cigarette and laughed. He thought about Rose. The girl he had left behind.

Chapter 5

A S HE DROVE home from his dad's house that Sunday afternoon, Sam reflected on the conversation he had just had with his father. He had asked Sam to take him to the reunion in DC, but Sam had hesitated.

Sam went over the reasons. Not only was the event in less than two weeks, but they still had to pack up the house in time for his move to the senior center. Plus, Sam worried about his dad's health and ability to travel. On top of all that, Sam was thinking about work and what he would miss by taking his dad on the trip. Sam was managing one of the most significant litigation cases in his office. It was a bad time to take a trip, even just for a few days.

He could hear his dad repeat his position about the event. "Son, I'm going, whether you take me or not."

Sam knew that he wasn't going to have much choice. He just needed to figure out how to do it. He lived ten minutes from his father's house or, as he would otherwise describe it, the house he grew up in. Nashville was a small suburban city. His mom and dad had lived there most of their lives, and Sam and his brother Ben had grown up there. About ten years ago, after many years away in New York, Sam had decided to move his family back. His return had made his parents happy. His older brother Ben had also come back, but under different circumstances. Sam had come back as the successful one. Ben had been the one who came back trying to "find himself."

Sam parked the car and walked into his house through the garage entrance. The house Sam had bought when they moved back to

Nashville was larger than what they could afford in New York. The house was in a well-regarded subdivision, close to the best schools that Nashville could offer.

"Lynn, I'm home," Sam announced, assuming his wife would hear him wherever she was in the house as long as he was loud enough.

"I'm upstairs," she replied.

"I'll be up soon." On instinct, he walked into the kitchen and opened the refrigerator to grab a bottle of water. His eyes glanced through the shelves, hoping to find something sweet, a reward after the day he had endured with his dad while packing up the house. He pulled out a Tupperware container and pursued his curiosity. Sam felt disappointed but not surprised when the container revealed to only contain vegetables. Since their children Aaron and Lucy had grown up and moved out, there were never any snacks in the fridge. He and Lynn had been empty nesters for more than six years.

He grabbed a bottle of water and closed the refrigerator. He began his march upstairs, trying to figure out how he would explain to his wife what his father wanted to do.

In the stairwell, he looked at the family pictures on the wall. There were pictures of him and Lynn and family portraits of Aaron and Lucy when they were younger. There were also pictures of his family with his parents. He looked at his mom's face. It had been five years already. Losing his mother had been hard for everyone, but nothing close to what it had done to his dad.

"Hi, honey," Sam said as he walked into the room. Lynn was in her closet.

"News from the front," Sam said as he sat on their bed and collapsed against the pillows that decorated the headboard.

She appeared from the closet, half-dressed.

"What are you doing?" Sam asked.

"Trying clothes on. There are things in my closet I never wear."

Sam wondered if that was because he was usually too tired to take her anywhere.

"How's your dad? How's the packing coming?" she asked as she finished putting on some old sweats for the rest of their Sunday night.

"You ready for this?" Sam hesitated, trying to build excitement.

"No. Sounds like I'm not." Lynn replied, familiar with her husband's approach to telling stories.

"He wants to go to DC for a reunion of his ship from World War II."

"Reunion?' the question lingered as she asked what seemed to be the obvious follow-up. "Is there anyone left?"

Sam tried to explain his father's words about the event. "Dad told me that he has not gone to any reunion since his discharge, but it sounds like he has some unfinished business. Come on, he's ninety years old. How do I say no to him for something like this? It sounds really important to him."

"When is this supposed to happen?" she asked.

"May eleventh," he replied.

"That's in two weeks!" She gave Sam a curious look, then walked over to her dresser and picked up her laptop. She climbed into bed, adjusting the throw pillows behind her. She then opened up her computer to research flights. "Is it even safe for him to travel…to manage from the car through the terminal to the plane?" She asked while she searched the travel sites.

"He's still using his walker and refuses to use a wheelchair," Sam said.

"So, you'll need to leave for the airport at least a week before your flight to give him time to walk the concourse." Lynn's sarcasm was showing through.

"Very funny," Sam said. "Won't be as funny when you and I are racing our walkers at the retirement home," he grinned at his wife. They had been married over thirty years already.

"The flights are ridiculously expensive. Direct flights are over twelve hundred dollars for economy." She kept searching. "What about driving?" she suggested.

"From Nashville to DC? What is that-eight hours?" Sam asked.

Lynn again checked the information online. "Ten," she responded.

"But that's at the speed limit. We both know you drive slower than that." She laughed.

"Again, not funny," he said. "Ten hours in the car with my dad?"

"You can make it a road trip. We'll find a nice place for you to stay overnight on the way there and on the way back. It will be a great chance for you to spend some quality time together."

Then she added, "It really might be easier than managing through an airport and renting a car." She seemed captivated by the idea of organizing a nice travel experience for them.

"You want to come with?" Sam asked.

"I would," Lynn said. "But sounds like it's a trip for two." She flashed a crooked smile.

Sam looked at his wife. She looked the same to him as the day they got married. He knew better than to disagree with her. One thing he knew: she was always right. He hated that. But there were things she just intuitively understood that he didn't. And therefore, just like that, Sam knew that in less than two weeks, he and his dad would be taking a long-overdue trip together.

"Road trip," Sam said out loud with a bit of sarcasm.

His wife leaned over the bed, kissed him, and said, "Have a nice time."

Chapter 6

THE CARRIER WAS dry-docked for almost two months undergoing the repairs and retrofits it needed before going back into battle. The damage to the ship from the multiple air assaults it suffered had taken its toll. In addition to repairs, sailors reinforced the bulkhead and the hanger deck with new steel to protect the Bunker Hill from air artillery and underwater torpedoes.

After finishing their work on the pilot house, Max and Tony helped add armor to the two gunner bays in the carrier's bow. The crew had also worked overtime in readying the ship with new anti-aircraft weaponry, including four new twin five-inch, 130-millimeter guns and eight quadruple forty-millimeter guns. These massive cannons would challenge the enemy aircraft that filled the air defending the Japanese home islands. The improvements to the ship were crucial. Like all aircraft carriers in the Pacific, the Bunker Hill made a large target for the enemy. They needed to be prepared to defend themselves.

While he was in Bremerton, five letters arrived. Two were from his mother and the rest were from Rose. Each night, when he tried to fall asleep over the sounds of his crewmates around him in their bunks, he reread Rose's letters.

Max knew he was in trouble the first time he saw her. She was walking down the stairwell in his mother's Brooklyn apartment building wearing a blue dress with white knee socks and black and white shoes. Her hair was down, and it flowed across her shoulders as she moved, like she was bouncing along clouds. Her eyes were brown, and Max watched her as she passed by him. He stuttered when he said "Hi," and she responded with a quick, "Hi to you, too!" as she disappeared down the remaining steps.

Max hesitated for a moment and then clumsily dropped some of the fruit and vegetables he had just brought at the market as he peered down the stairwell to catch another glimpse of her. She was almost to the bottom. When she reached the landing, she looked up at Max and sped out the door.

After he caught his breath, Max picked up the dropped groceries. He fumbled with his keys at their apartment door before rushing inside. His mother was in the kitchen as he laid down the torn bag of groceries.

"Don't bruise the fruit," his mother said.

Max wasn't listening. He was still thinking about the girl who had floated past him on the stairs.

"Mom?" Max framed her name as a question that he had yet to form in his head. "I just saw a girl. Dark hair, coming down from the fifth floor. Do you know who she is?"

His mother was a well-known gossip in the building. "It must be the Katz's granddaughter," she said. "She's visiting from Connecticut. She's in school there." His mother was always right.

"You know her name?" Max asked.

"Rose," She said.

But before she could turn around and ask why, Max had grabbed his keys and was out the door. He had to find her.

Chapter 7

L YNN HAD GROWN up in Knoxville, but she was working in Nashville at the same time that Sam was in law school at Georgetown. He was home visiting one weekend to celebrate his parent's wedding anniversary and had gone out with some buddies to a local bar when mutual friends introduced them. They had spent that night talking and then spent the next night at her apartment. He fell hard for her.

Since she was working in Nashville, they got to see each other every time he visited home from law school, and they spent more time together during the long breaks between semesters. He finally brought her home to meet his parents in the spring of his third year of school. He had waited to make the introduction since she wasn't Jewish, and he wasn't sure how his parents would react. When they met Lynn, they were warm and welcoming. But Sam didn't know what they might be saying behind his back. Whatever it was, Sam understood. His parents were both rooted in their religion. The concept of religious intermarriage was challenging. His parents still felt anxious about how the Holocaust had reduced the number of Jews in the world; this intermarriage would not help to change that.

When Sam told his father that he was planning to propose, his father had asked, "Are you sure?"

Max was less concerned about his father than he was about his mother. She had grown up in a traditional Jewish family and lost many family members in eastern Europe during the war.

"Marriage is hard," his father had said. "You have to be compatible.

There are already enough differences to deal with. The more you see things the same way, the easier it will be."

Max had asked Sam if he was "happy." When Sam said "Yes," that was all his father needed to hear. But he told Sam it might "take a while" for Rose to come around. "Give her time," he would say.

Sam and Lynn dated long-distance for the rest of Sam's last semester at school. At first, Sam thought he would return to Tennessee to work, so he took the Tennessee bar exam when he graduated. He even got an offer from a firm in Nashville that his parents were excited for him to accept. But before he started work that fall, another offer came from a bigger firm in New York.

Lynn said that she was willing to move with Sam to New York. She wanted to be with him. But Sam wondered if her willingness to relocate also had to do with his parents. It's not as if his mother had not accepted Lynn into the family. He just felt as if there was always an underlying tension. His mother would often say "well, she just doesn't understand" as a clear slight to her different background. Sam would never admit that it was this chasm between his parents and Lynn over religion that led him to move away, but he recognized that it was a part of it.

So, they moved to New York after he graduated. Sam took the New York bar exam and started work. They got married a year later. Lynn didn't convert but they agreed to raise their children to be Jewish. The wedding was in Knoxville at a local event facility. No rabbi, no priest, just a justice of the peace. Sam still stomped on a glass at the end of the ceremony to "scare away any demons" that may have been around them. They honeymooned on a cruise in the Caribbean and then flew back to New York to start their lives. It would take them twenty years to move back.

Chapter 8

MAX AND TONY were excited to hear they would receive their last shore leave on New Year's Eve. Although some crewmen would take ferries into Seattle, Max, Tony, and their crewmates took a cab into downtown Bremerton, where the bars would overflow with sailors and the naval yard shipbuilders who had moved there to help with the war effort.

That night, the men granted shore leave gathered at the top of the wooden walkway leading from the ship to waiting cabs. As they signed off with the guards overseeing access and departures from the ship, Max and Tony hailed one of the cabs and squeezed in with two fellow sailors.

"Take us to where the action is!" Tony belted out in his distinct New Jersey Italian voice.

"I know what you guys are looking for!" the driver responded.

The four sailors laughed. The men were each thirsty for some drinking and, some hopefully, to find sex before they returned to the ship and eventually took their chances against the Japanese. Even without saying it out loud, they each knew that not all of them would make it back. They each had known men who had died in the war, some at sea against the Japanese and others on the battlefields in Europe. But, to a man, each knew it was a noble fight. And, if they didn't make it, an honorable death.

When the clock struck midnight to start 1945, Max and Tony were already three sheets to the wind in a bar. They knew that as the calendar page turned to January, it would not be long before the

Bunker Hill was released back into the fray. They all realized what their next step would be. To push the American armada toward Japan for an assault on Tokyo. The booze flowed freely, each drink to try to erase the worry that each of the men faced as they considered the enemy that faced them in the Western Pacific.

"Happy New Year," the men said as they raised their beers to salute one other. The men were not naïve. Still, none of them had any idea what awaited.

It was close to three in the morning when Max found an unoccupied payphone. He deposited all the change in his pocket and dialed her number from memory. It would be almost six in the morning on the East Coast.

Rose picked up on the second ring. "Hello?" she whispered, not wanting to wake her parents.

"Rose. It's Max." Max was drunk. The words sloshed together.

"Max," her voice was buoyed. "How are you?"

"Happy New Year," he said. And then he repeated when she did not respond. "Happy New Year."

"Happy New Year to you, too," she replied, still smiling at the sound of Max's voice.

"We ship out in a few weeks," Max tried to explain in a serious tone. "We leave for Tokyo!"

"I miss you," she answered, not wanting to think of Max's deployment.

"I'll be home one day soon." Max said.

"I know." Rose said. There was sadness in her voice.

"Soon." Max said again. "And then we'll get married."

"I'll wait for you, Max," Rose said. "I'll wait for you."

Max moved the receiver away from his face and repositioned his arms against the wall of the booth, trying to hold himself up. He suddenly felt sick. He wanted to be home. It struck him that he might not make it back. "Wish me luck, Rose," He asked her.

"I love you," was all she said.

Max and Rose had been inseparable before Max had left for

basic training. He had wanted to propose to her before he left, but he didn't think it was the right thing to do. He already knew too many young widows. He promised her that when he came back that they would get married. It was this promise that he thought would keep him alive.

Chapter 9

I T WAS MONDAY morning, and Sam had not slept well. He had known he would have a busy week, and now there was a new item on his to-do list: planning his trip with his dad. Sam never slept well on Sunday nights anyway, filled with the dread of the work week beginning once again, just as it had for over thirty years of his legal practice.

Sometimes, when he said "thirty years" out loud, he surprised himself with his longevity. For some reason, he had grown up imagining that if he worked somewhere for twenty-five years, he would get a gold watch and retire. He had saved for that retirement, somewhat. He had done fine, but not nearly as well as friends who had invested in real estate or built equity with their companies. He considered himself the tortoise of his friends: slow but steady.

He had undoubtedly saved money by moving back to Nashville from Westchester. The cost of living in New York was ridiculous. Sam knew he would never have survived that. But again, the lawyers at his old firm were making twice what he was. The compensation was higher because the hourly rates were higher, but so were the monthly billable requirements. Sam had jumped from that rat race ten years ago. He might have had some regrets, but they were only about money. His life in Nashville was better for all of them. The work was more reasonable. And he was able to be back with his parents. When his mother passed, the importance of his presence hit home. But he especially appreciated being part of his father's day-to-day life since then.

This morning, he stopped on the way to work to grab a coffee at Starbucks. He sat in his car to take a few sips before continuing his commute. Sam was lucky. The total drive was less than thirty minutes.

He parked in his usual parking garage spot and made his way to the lobby of the forty-story building, one of the tallest in downtown Nashville. Sam had been taking the elevator to the same floor in the same building to the same office for the last ten years. Even at sixty, Sam still billed more than most of the other partners at the firm. In many ways, once he started his billable clock every day, it was hard to turn it off. There was always something else to do; if Sam wasn't working on billable work, he was marketing to existing or new clients. He understood that the only currency he had with his firm was the work that he brought in. He always worried about the job, even when he didn't need to. He was at a point in his career when he shouldn't need to worry, but he still did.

Since Aaron and Lucy had left the house for college, he had started working even more. When the kids were growing up, he occasionally tried to leave early for a game or a recital. Now, he didn't have those excuses. If Lynn didn't prod him each year, he wasn't sure he would even take time off for vacations. As he pushed open the glass doors and murmured "Good morning" to the receptionist, Sam knew he was now at a point where he'd been sucked too far down the vacuum. It was hard to get out. Work had become all-consuming. He hated it, but it was who he was. It was clients, lawsuits, trials, appeals, reboot, and restart. Every one-tenth of an hour was billed.

The next few weeks would be more of the same. A class-action lawsuit had been filed against one of the firm's clients, a pharmaceutical company, for allegedly dispensing a cold medicine that caused blood clots in teenagers. There had been four deaths, and the trial was only a few weeks away.

It was Sam's job to coordinate more than a dozen partners and associates to manage the discovery, documents, depositions, trial preparation, and so forth. He sat in his office or at the head of the large conference table, leading this well-dressed orchestra, each following their own page of sheet music to create the symphony of a defense team for trial. If someone went off-key, missed a beat, switched their sheet music, or failed to follow his baton in any way, the case would crash.

Sam would be blamed—and he feared failure. He feared being discovered that maybe he was only as good as the second-chair cellist instead of a true conductor. His career would burn to the ground, and he would be kicked to the curb. Imposter syndrome. What if, after thirty years of practicing law, he was found not to be as bright and confident as he had seemed? As the years went on, Sam just hoped he could finish his career without being discovered. He just hoped to save enough for his retirement before being found out.

He wasn't sure where this neurosis came from. His parents had not pushed him. They were always supportive. Maybe it was because they didn't demand anything from him that he wanted to succeed for them. Sam also wanted their lives to be easier with him. They had already been through some rough times with his older brother Ben. Even if it wasn't expected, Sam always was trying to make amends for the actions of his brother.

As he got older, Sam just wanted to continue to achieve, first for Lynn and then for Aaron and Lucy. He felt like it was his responsibility to be successful. That it was what he was "supposed" to do, so he did it. He worked to succeed as if he didn't have a choice. But it came at a cost. He was never really at home. He always had a conflict. He had to work.

Sam sat down at his desk and studied the invitation that his dad had given him. Sam exhaled at the stress of dealing with this last-minute issue for his dad and tried to imagine how difficult the trip would be. The host was listed as the American Veterans Association. He dialed the number.

"Good morning," a young woman's voice resonated through the phone. "American Veterans Association. How can I help you?"

Sam hesitated. He still wasn't convinced that this trip should happen. But he had already started. "Hi. I'm calling about the Bunker Hill reunion event on May eleventh. Is there someone at the Association I can talk to about the event? It's about one of the veterans who was invited."

"Certainly. Let me look up the program. You said May eleventh? Which event?"

"Bunker Hill. To be held at the World War II Memorial."

"Of course. I see it. Let me connect you to Stephen Henton. He's the coordinator for the program."

"Perfect," Sam said. "Thank you." He heard the phone ringing at the new location.

"Hello. This is Steve Henton. How can I help you?" The voice was strong but old. Sam wondered if he was a veteran himself.

"Mr. Henton, my name is Sam Silver. My dad was on the USS Bunker Hill. You're doing a reunion event on May 11 for the ship at the World War II Memorial. He was on the invite list."

"Okay, let me pull that up. Give me a second to find it." Sam began to understand that this was just one of probably dozens of events this group handled.

"Got it. Here it is. And yes. I see your dad's name. He's not on our RSVP list. Is he okay?"

"Yes. Yes. For a guy who's ninety, he is still going strong."

"Good to hear. So, how can I help?"

"It's about the invite. He only just decided to attend. Is it too late?" Sam was hoping that the event had been sold out and he would not have to make the trip.

Henton did not hesitate. "No. Not at all. We'd be honored to have him. As you can imagine, since we did this event ten years ago for the sixtieth anniversary, we have lost a number of our veterans. It would be wonderful if he could attend."

"So, what do we need to do to reserve his spot?"

"Consider it done," Henton replied. He added, "How many family members will be joining him?"

"Just me."

"If you give me your e-mail, Mr. Silver, I will send you the specifics."

"Sorry about the late response," Sam added.

"Well, as they say…" Henton hesitated, "better late than never."

Sam chuckled. It was an expression that his father always used.

After Sam hung up with the veteran's office, he got up and started down the hall to talk to one of his partners about his planned trip. He wanted everyone to know that this wasn't a vacation. He convinced himself that he would only be out of pocket from Friday until Monday. Case preparation would still happen without him, but he knew he needed to do this. It was time to let some things go.

The trip added one more thing to his growing list of responsibilities: work, home, Lynn, the kids, friends, and just "stuff," all of which always seemed to overtake the moment and remove his ability to be present. Nothing was ever really too urgent or important, but it always seemed overwhelming and distracting at the moment. Now he was adding another thing to that list. It worried him, but he also accepted it.

It had been too long since he had spent real one-on-one time with his dad. The years were fleeting. He knew that. The old joke that "Dad won't be around forever" wasn't as funny anymore since it was true. When his dad turned ninety, it seemed to be a bit of a miracle. He had gotten older, of course, slower. But he was still "Dad." And Sam had always been curious about his father's time in the military.

Sam never had to face war. He'd grown up in the "no war" cycle of history in the seventies and eighties. It was post-Vietnam, when the country realized that war wasn't glamorous or easy. Sure, Nixon, Carter, and Reagan had challenged Russia to avoid blowing each other up, but nothing had really happened. Instead, the countries realized they could focus on economic growth and success if they didn't spend all of their money at war. There was no war, no bloodshed in our lives. Only opportunity and freedom. MTV, *Happy Days*, and *Dallas*. When he was twenty, Sam was in college. When his dad was twenty, he was on an aircraft carrier in the Pacific. Sam never risked his life. His dad had.

Once he convinced himself that the trip would happen, Sam was all-in. The trip would be a way to relate to his dad, connect and share something with him as significant as the war his dad had fought seventy years before. He was a bit fascinated with all of it. Of course, Sam had read over the years about the war. He understood the threat of Hitler, the expansion in Europe, the domination of the Japanese in the east, and the shifting power of Russia. He had read about the tens of millions who had died. But it was just that: what he had read. His only real connection to World War II was his father. As a veteran, his dad had always served as proof that it had happened, but nothing more.

Sam could never really understand what it must have been like for his father to go to war when he was only twenty, and Sam thought he could connect further with his dad on this trip, but he went into it naively. He wanted to share his dad's experience and learn from him, but his dad had not really talked about the war when Sam was growing up, and now, he didn't quite know what he would find.

Chapter 10

THE BUNKER HILL departed from the Port of Bremerton and the Navy Shipyard on January 24, 1945. As it steamed its way west, the waves crashed alongside the massive aircraft carrier at a speed of thirty knots as its four turbines propelled the ship through rough seas heading toward the East China Sea. Along with its recent upgrades, the Bunker Hill had fortified itself with a squadron of new Grumman F6F Hellcats fighters and a new set of experienced pilots. The Bunker Hill would be the flagship for Task Force 58, commanded by Vice Admiral Marc Mitscher. After more than three years at war with Japan, the United States Pacific Fifth Fleet was beginning its final push against the Imperial Japanese Navy forces. The carrier was scheduled to rejoin the Fleet for its final attack to control the Japanese home islands.

As the ship pushed west, the off-duty crew played cards or wrote long letters to their families back home. Most understood that they were entering the most terrifying part of their service but knew they could also be part of the final campaign to win the war against Japan.

Having completed his training, Max assumed full duty as a radar operator in the Combatant Information Center or "CIC." He was excited about the assignment because the CIC was considered part of the "brains" of the aircraft carrier. The CIC used the carrier's radar systems to spot enemy aircraft in the area. If they saw anything on the radar, the CIC would pass the word to man battle stations and notify the pilots. The ship was always ready for an attack. Max's job was to watch the radar screen to identify any "bogies" or unidentified objects. He acted as the eyes for the ship. He knew that people would die if he missed anything on the radar. He also knew he depended on machines, which were not always perfect.

That night had been a calm night in the Pacific. Max had overheard the commanders in the CIC discuss their position and their movement along with the fleet. Within a week, they were almost halfway to their target, the islands south of Japan, and would arrive within days. When he was relieved from his shift, Max climbed the metal stairs from the CIC, which was below the flight deck, up to the command tower. He tried to light a cigarette. The wind extinguished his matches.

"Here, try this," a voice said, and someone handed him a lighter. Max put his back to the wind and lit his cigarette.

Max then recognized his friend. "Hey, Tony. Thanks. What are you doing up here?"

"Had to take a break," his friend said. "Thought I'd find you." Tony had been assigned as a gunner's mate, the same role he'd played on the USS Massachusetts. Tony managed one of the five-inch 38-caliber artillery guns. The work was tedious but important. If a plane were spotted, the crew would have little time to shoot it down before it attacked. The large armaments were the ship's primary defense against an aerial assault.

"Another couple of days before the fun starts," Max said to Tony.

"Oh yeah? Thought we were already having fun."

Max laughed and took a strong draw from his cigarette. The nicotine kept him alert. "Iwo Jima," he said.

"That's what I figured. I heard we were loading the planes heavy," Tony responded, explaining the size of the bombs the planes were carrying. "The air groups will carpet bomb the islands before the Marines land. We need to wipe out the higher positions."

Max didn't respond. He just nodded.

"Don't worry, buddy. You'll see her again. You're a sailor. No one shoots at sailors," Tony quipped. "We just drive the boats." He knew Max was thinking about Rose.

"Funny," Max replied.

"We're almost done," Tony said to cheer his friend up. "Story is that we are winning in Germany. Now, if we can only get Japan to wise up, we can all go home."

Max answered, "I don't get it. They have to know they're going to lose. The entire Fifth Fleet is heading their way. The Task Force has eighteen battleships, dozens of cruisers, over 150 destroyers, and forty aircraft carriers. Over 100,000 marines and infantry."

"It's all about honor," said Tony. "They will fight until they die."

Chapter 11

AFTER WORK ON Tuesday, Sam dropped by to see his dad. He wanted to update him on the plan for the trip. As he and Lynn had discussed, they would drive rather than fly. It would take them over ten hours to make the trip, assuming a bunch of stops along the way. Lynn and Sam had figured out that they would drive to Charlottesville on Friday, which would be about eight hours, and then spend the night there. Then they could get up on Saturday morning and drive the two to three hours to DC in time for the reunion that started at one o'clock. They would spend the night in DC on Saturday after the event and then start back to Nashville on Sunday. Sam was hoping to manage the entire drive in a single day so he could make it to the office Monday morning and only miss just one day of work.

Sam repeated the driving plan to his father. "Dad. It will be a fun road trip! It's been a long time since the two of us have taken a trip together." But Sam didn't recall if they had ever taken a trip together.

"I guess that's fine," Max acknowledged, adding sternly, "As long as we'll be there in time for the reunion."

"Yes. Absolutely. But, Dad, here's the bargain. I agree to take you for the reunion; you agree to cooperate and move into the center."

His father stared at his son without blinking.

"It's hospice," his father quietly reacted. "It's where people go to die."

Sam was a bit stunned. "Of course not," he said defensively. "It's an independent living center. We're just worried about you being in the house alone without us. What if something happens?" It was quiet for a few moments when Sam added to his argument. "Dad. We'll move your own furniture into the apartment. All that will be different is that you'll be able to have your meals made. And they'll be someone there at any hour if you need anything."

Sam was selling.

Max understood the deal. He wasn't going to battle with his son over the move to the center. It wasn't worth the fight. "Sure," he said, adding, "Life is full of bargains."

"But," Sam finished, "your doctor still needs to give you the green light to travel."

"Fine. My appointment is Thursday. And I like my doctor. She's sort of cute."

Max laughed. "Only a ninety-year-old can say that."

"I guess," his father said. "Age does have its privileges."

Sam smiled. "Hey, Dad, I'm going upstairs to work on packing up one of the bedrooms. Want to help?"

"No. I'm a bit tired. I'm going to watch some TV if that's all right."

"Sure, Dad." Sam grabbed a packing box and headed upstairs. He walked into the room that had been his bedroom growing up. It felt smaller to him. Someone had packed away much of his stuff years before—but books, framed photos, and assorted memorabilia lined the shelves, and the closet was filled with old clothes that had not been worn in decades. Sam started a "save" pile, and a "donate" pile. The "donate" pile grew larger by the minute.

As he started to pack some of the pictures, he came across an old family photo: his parents, Sam, and his brother Ben. He tried to remember where it had been taken. They were all outside. The leaves in the trees in the background were turning color for the Fall. His parents were sitting, and Ben and Sam were standing behind them. He stared into the image to attempt to relive the moment, looking closely at the faces of the four of them. So many years ago. So much had happened. He thought about his mom. He thought about his brother. He had lost them both. It was just him and his dad now.

Sam looked at his mom's face with that broad smile. She loved her family. There was no doubt in the world that the greatest joy in her life was when she was surrounded by her loving husband and two children. Her family was her life's work, her ultimate masterpiece.

He had fought to keep his memories of her clear in his mind over the last five years since her death, but so much of his past was fading. It upset Sam that he had a tough time remembering his youth. But he still felt tremendous love for his mother. She had always been there for him. He would have flashes of memories of the times he rode in the backseat of her car on the way to school or when she would go shopping with him to buy him clothes. He remembered how she would make him his lunches for school and how she would leave notes for him in his lunchbox. He remembered her laughter and sense of joy when he was growing up. And he remembered her courage when she got sick.

He looked at his brother in the picture. He still couldn't believe he was gone. Sam was still angry about what had happened, but that was only to mask his sadness. He missed him. He missed his zest for life, the twinkle in his eye.

He looked at their faces in the picture one more time and smiled. But Sam knew that the rest of his life would not be the same without his mother and his brother. Sam held onto the picture and closed the packing box. He would be keeping this photo for himself.

Chapter 12

THE FIFTH FLEET began its final assault against the Japanese under a plan called "Operation Detachment." The Battle of Iwo Jima would start on February 16, 1945. The armada of destroyers, battleships, and carriers would support the pre-invasion bombing of the island to destroy any bunker installations or gun emplacements that were defending the beach. Then, the planes from the Bunker Hill and other carriers would fly overhead to provide cover fire for the Marines landing on the island. The planes would also conduct strafing and bombing runs to destroy any aircraft on the ground and their hangers, including any known aircraft factories.

Max and his crewmates understood that the goal of the Allied forces in taking Iwo Jima was to create a unique strategic opportunity. Once the island was secured, they would then be able to embark on "Operation Downfall," the eventual invasion of Tokyo. They all realized that once islands like Iwo Jima were captured, bomber raids could be based closer to Tokyo. The flight distance would be cut in half, and the damage to the Japanese capital would be more intensive.

When he was relieved of duty for rest breaks, Max would often go and stand along the railings on the flight deck and survey the movement of the armada of ships that surrounded the island. The vessels carried the tens of thousands of Marine and Army personnel who would be part of the landing.

As he rested against the metal structure, he watched the waves crash below as the carrier moved to the west of the island to obtain strategic advantage. Fellow crew members moved around him as they watched together the hellcats and corsairs leave the ship one after another to support the ongoing attack.

"This is the beginning of their end," one of the crew members yelled above the sound of the plane engines behind him. "They can't beat us!"

But Max knew that the battle had just begun.

Chapter 13

O N THURSDAY MORNING, Lynn picked up Max to drive him to his appointment at the VA Hospital. As part of his government benefits, Max was afforded free medical treatment at the local Veteran's Administration Hospital, which was staffed with government doctors and was used as a training facility for nearby medical schools like Vanderbilt. The hospital was too small, understaffed, and frequently overwhelmed by its mission: to treat veterans who had served their country during World War II, Korea, Vietnam, Iran, Iraq, and Afghanistan, not to mention all the nation's peacekeeping missions. Thousands of veterans of all ages, experiencing a range of physical and mental medical challenges, made their way through the doors. The staff of nurses and doctors were consistently overwhelmed with the patient load but somehow still managed to treat the needs of the veterans, some of whom traveled hours to get there. Max was lucky. He had been in the system for decades and was a "regular" with a terrific group of doctors that cared for him.

But there was never any parking.

Lynn drove up to the main entrance. Max unbuckled his seatbelt and opened the passenger-side door to leave. Lynn surveyed the patients gathered outside of the building entrance. Most were smoking, even in designated "No smoking" areas. By their appearance, these were the soldiers and sailors who had spent time in Vietnam, much older and grayer than the men and women who had returned from Iran, Iraq, and Afghanistan. The Vietnam vets, from Lynn's perspective, was the misunderstood generation of those servicemen and woman that had fought for a lost cause and returned to a country that didn't understand loss. There were fewer and fewer World War II veterans at the hospital. Most of the servicemembers that Max had known had long since passed on.

"I'll need to drive around and find a parking spot," Lynn said to her father-in-law as she pulled his walker from the back of the car. "It might take me a while. I'll meet you in the doctor's office."

"Fine, Lynn. Fine," said Max without looking back. He was used to the routine. Any time Sam took him to his appointment, they suffered the same fate. Max was already starting his long, slow walk into the hospital lobby, aided by his walker.

Lynn felt terrible that she had to drop Max off at the front of the hospital and then drive around to find a place to park. There was never any room in the parking decks. She sat in the car waiting while she watched Max slowly make his way into the building. While she watched, she called Sam on her cellphone. He wasn't surprised by her call. He knew what to expect when he heard from her. He had taken Max to most of his appointments. He knew how frustrating it could be.

"This is crazy," she said to her husband. "He can afford to go to a private doctor. I don't understand why he wants to go here."

"Sorry, honey," Sam calmly responded. "Thank you for taking him."

"It's a mess here. People are just waiting. And the smoking. It's a hospital, for crying out loud!" She was exasperated.

She drove the car around the corner to the new parking deck that had just opened a few months ago. A red neon light already showed it as "Full."

Lynn realized that eventually, she wouldn't be able to just drop Max off in front, not without more help. And she knew the walker was temporary. He would soon need a wheelchair to get through the hospital. She expressed her concern to Sam. Then she told him she would call him back after the appointment to tell him what the doctor said.

He again thanked her for taking his dad to the appointment.

Lynn knew that it was hard for Sam. He was trying to balance work while at the same time trying to care for his family and for his dad. He was doing the best that he could. She knew it wasn't easy for him. Sam would always say that "life sometimes gives you a full plate."

"Love you," Sam said.

"You, too. I will call you later." Lynn ended the call as she drove out of the hospital parking lot and turned down the street toward a commercial office complex. Although the signs at the entrance warned against unauthorized parking in the office building parking lot, she had yet to be ticketed or towed.

Lynn had ensured, as she always did, that they left with plenty of time to make the appointment. Enough time especially if she could not find parking at the hospital, and she was forced to park at this lot, which was easily half a mile from the hospital entrance. She had to walk back to meet Max. It was hot and humid. Lynn felt like rain was coming. As she walked, she realized that she had not dressed properly for this possibility.

Today, Max was seeing his internist, Dr. Han. She was a recent graduate of the University of Tennessee Medical School and was doing her residency in geriatric medicine at the VA. Max was one of her more elderly patients.

When Lynn found Max in the lobby, they began their long walk to her office. It took Max a while to make it to her office since he refused to use a wheelchair. He was adamant that he could make the trip with his walker. He had taken a few falls over the last year but had not broken anything.

"We called Dr. Han to tell her about the upcoming trip. We just wanted to make sure you would be okay to make the drive," Lynn reminded her father-in-law.

"I'm fine, Lynn. I am." Max said. "I'm happy that Sam is taking me. This trip is important."

Lynn and Max found their seats in the waiting area after Lynn gave Max's name to the receptionist.

"Hi, Mr. Silver," the nurse said. The staff knew Max well. He smiled in response.

Their appointment was scheduled for ten o'clock, but Lynn knew they always ran late. Too many patients and not enough doctors. Today would be no exception.

Chapter 14

TADAMICHI KURIBAYASHI WAS the Japanese General charged with defending Iwo Jima. What the Americans didn't know was that in the months preceding the attack, Kuribayashi had coordinated his forces to build an extensive system of tunnels, bunkers, and command centers into the island. Some were as many as ninety feet deep and they extended more than eleven miles in length. The Allies had unloaded tons of bombs and heavy naval gunfire before invading forces even arrived, but these had only minimally impacted the thousands of Japanese defending the island. By the time the Marines landed at Iwo Jima, 450 American ships were stationed off the island. More than 100,000 Marines and infantry would make the assault, but they had no idea what awaited them.

Max heard from other crew members about the brutal combat that was happening on the island. The pilots who returned acknowledged that the Americans were making little headway against the embedded Japanese forces. It sounded as if for every advancement made, the Japanese would retreat to their underground tunnels and reappear behind the advance forces, cutting them down without warning.

Max heard the stories of whole battalions being wiped out during midnight raids by the Japanese. Using their tunnels, the enemy would emerge from their hidden underground bunkers in the dark of night to surround and surprise the Marines. The enemy apparently gave the soldiers no chance to surrender.

At night, Max wrote to Rose about what he had heard. His

letters shared his fears about the war and the atrocities that had been shared with him. He didn't want to worry her, but he did want to prepare her. Ships had been sunk. Sailors had been killed. The stench of death surrounded him. He wrote by flashlight as the men around him slept. If he were to die, he wanted her to know that he had thought about her and their future together. Those were the thoughts that kept him going: dreams about being back home and being together. He thought about what his life would be like after the war, how many children they would have, where they would live, and how they would grow old together.

Chapter 15

S AM GOT HOME late Thursday night. He didn't have much time during the day to talk to Lynn about his dad's appointment. It had been a busy day. The class action case took up most of his time at the office. He would have to work at home tonight and was expecting to work over the weekend, too. He was trying to wrap up as much as possible before the DC trip, hoping it wouldn't be a big deal for him to be out of pocket.

As he walked inside, he dropped his files on the couch and went to their liquor cabinet to pour himself a bourbon. He called out to Lynn, who was in the kitchen.

"You want anything? I am in crisis mode to have this drink. Scary thing is that I've been thinking about it all day," he half-joked.

"No. I'm going to have some wine," she said. "Or I should clarify and say *more* wine."

Sam walked into the kitchen carrying his drink. "Tough day at the VA Hospital?" he asked, trying to lighten the mood.

"It is so sad there," said Lynn. "The long lines, the waiting. The system is so broken. All these veterans needing services and not enough help or attention for them." She took a deep breath. "We waited an hour after our appointment time to be seen and then another hour in the pharmacy waiting for his prescriptions to be filled. There has got to be a better way."

"No budget for veterans," Sam said.

"These are men and women who risked their lives for this country. Those that aren't killed come back either physically or mentally harmed." She took a big swig of her wine. "Why won't he just go to a private doctor? It would be easier for him and for us. It's not like he can't afford it."

"I think it's his pride for being a veteran, that it's a benefit for his service." Sam answered. Then he said, "Plus he's cheap." Sam laughed.

Lynn was not amused.

"What did they say? Can he go on the trip?" Sam asked. Once again, he was hoping for a reason to cancel.

"Good try, honey. She said he's fine to travel. She got him another prescription to help his blood flow when he's sitting in the car for a long duration. You'll need to make whatever stops you can so he can stretch and go to the bathroom."

"So, I'll be traveling with you?" he laughed. "Smallest bladder in Tennessee?"

"Very funny," she said. Then she smiled. "She suggested he could also wear a diaper."

"Crap!" Sam said. "You have got to be kidding me. Can we please talk about something else?"

"How about the fact that your dad was hitting on his thirty-year-old doctor? He thinks she's cute."

"Yeah, I know," Sam replied. "Great, I'll try to find a hooker for him in DC too." He was kidding but also getting frustrated at the thought of trying to make his dad behave as his inhibitions diminished with age.

Sam and Lynn sat down for dinner. Lynn had picked up some food from a vegetarian place she had started to frequent. Sam joked that they must have been "investors" since they ate there so regularly—but he wasn't sure that she found this as funny as he did.

Their conversation, as always, turned to updates about their kids. Lynn shared with Sam that she had spoken to Lucy during the day and that their daughter would be coming home this weekend. She was finishing her first year of work toward a master's in social work at Duke.

Lynn added, "Her last final for the semester was yesterday."

"Terrific. It's been way too long since she's been home. Maybe she'll help me do some packing at my dad's house on Sunday. I have to go into the office Saturday."

"Why don't you call her later? It would be nice for you to talk to her."

"I will." Sam was unhappy that he needed a reminder from his wife to call his daughter.

Sam reflected on Lucy's path through college, her postgraduate work for a year in New York doing sales, and her decision to return south for her master's degree. Duke was a great school. He was proud of her and her goals.

"And Aaron. Have you spoken with him?" Sam asked as he moved from the kitchen table back to the bar to fill up his glass.

"Yes," Lynn said. A sadness in her voice. "Earlier in the week. You need to call him, too."

"Anything new?" Sam asked.

"No. But you just need to talk to him," she repeated. She sounded concerned.

"I know. I will," Sam said. "I need to go upstairs to work. Thanks for dinner."

Sam grabbed his files from the table and started to make his way up the stairs. Before he made it to the top of the stairs, he stopped. Sam leaned over the railing and called to his wife, who was still sitting at the kitchen table. "Is he okay?' Sam asked, nervous again for her answer.

"Please, just call him," she said. Sam heard the concern again in her voice.

Sam knew not to ask her anything more. He retreated up the remaining stairs. Sam had turned Aaron's room into his home office. Sam had moved everything from Aaron's desk and replaced it with a computer, printer, and a few family pictures. Still, he had otherwise left the room just as Aaron had decorated it before leaving for college. From where he sat, he could gaze up and see posters of athletes and bands thumbtacked to the walls. It made Sam feel closer to his son. But a lot had happened since Aaron left for college.

When he settled down at his desk, he organized the files he had brought home from the office and placed his drink on the coaster next to his computer. He took a deep breath, pulled out his phone, and dialed his daughter's number.

"Hey, Dad," came the buoyant voice on the other end.

"Hey, Luce," Sam replied. "How are you?"

"Great," she said. "Finished exams yesterday. Did Mom tell you I was coming home this weekend?"

"Yes. That's great. Can't wait to see you."

"I'm on my way out to meet some friends for dinner," she said. "We can catch up when I get home. Is that all right?" his daughter asked.

"Sure. Sounds great. Maybe you'll go with me to see Grandpa on Sunday. We're packing up the house."

"Sure," she said. "Sounds like a plan."

"Thanks, honey. See you soon. Please drive safe." Sam had to always include that when the kids were driving. Sam thought that maybe he had inherited that habit from his father.

"Bye, Dad."

Sam looked at his phone. There would never be a better time. He called Aaron's number. "Hey, it's Aaron." It was his son's voicemail. "Leave me a message or shoot me a text."

Sam left a message but struggled to find the right words. "I was just checking in. Hope you are doing okay. Would love to speak to you some time." He pressed the "end call" button on his phone. Sam shook his head thinking about his son.

Sam reflected on his last phone call with Aaron. Sam had tried to explain to Aaron his concerns. Sam had told him that one day, when Aaron had his own kids, he would understand his father's fears and protections. Sam tried to convince his son that being a parent was not always easy, but Aaron had been short with him, and the call had not ended well.

Sam turned to look at the framed pictures that he had placed on his makeshift desk. Pictures from family trips to the beach or the mountains He looked at his kids. All he had wanted was to teach them to be independent, happy, and move on to bigger and better lives. Sam took a long breath. Aaron was just doing what Sam had done. He had moved away from where his parents had lived to live his own life. Aaron was no different. But Sam didn't want to give up that easily. He was trying to make up for lost time and wanted to create a connection with his son that matched the bond that Sam felt he had with his father.

He gazed again at the pictures of his family. Sam smiled. At the end of the day, all that really mattered was his family. He didn't want to lose them. He had lost too much already.

Chapter 16

THE BATTLE FOR Iwo Jima lasted longer than the United States forces had anticipated. Max would watch his radar screen every day to follow the movement of the American fighters as they attacked the island and provided air support for the troops. But their efforts didn't seem to change the outcome. The losses were starting to mount. Max worried that the Allied forces had underestimated the resolve of the Japanese. Max reflected on his constant fear and anxious readiness, often wondering if he would even survive the war.

At times, the sounds on the ship were deafening. There was the general alarm, a ringing bell, which wailed its warning to all on deck. Then there were nearby battleships, exploding sixteen-inch fifty-caliber shells that pounded the beach, and anti-aircraft guns that sent bullets strafing across the sky to shield the incoming planes. As men ran from their bunks to their stations or from the ready rooms to the flight deck, their movements were silenced by the ear-splitting sounds. The intensity of the sounds matched the constant movement of the carrier as the heavy seas pushed and pulled it back and forth and up and down, sending many men to the railings to relieve their stomachs.

Max and Tony would meet regularly on the flight deck during their breaks to smoke or drink whiskey from the small flask that Tony hid in his coat. They knew that if they got caught drinking, they would end up in the brig, but it was worth it. Anything they could do to cut the tension. Each took a swig from the flask and then shared a stick of gum to hide the smell.

"Another day in paradise," Tony would often say.

"Beats working," Max joked. But the men knew that their lives were tenuous, even when the shelling stopped. What they were experiencing was unspoken, but each could see the fires raging on the island and knew that men were dying to fight for the control of Mount Suribachi, only 500 feet high but a strategic landmark on Iwo Jima.

Chapter 17

IT HAPPENED THE first time, or at least it was the first time that Sam and Lynn learned about it, during his last semester his senior year in college. Aaron had stopped going to classes and his grades tanked. The notice from the school then led to some tough conversations between Aaron and his parents about whether he should come home and drop out of school, but he convinced them that he would be able to do enough to pass his classes and graduate. The change in behavior troubled Sam and Lynn. They were worried that he was either partying too much or was suffering from depression. When they talked to him Aaron simply said that he felt "burnt out" and was struggling regularly with what he would be doing after he graduated.

Lynn and Sam would find themselves endlessly discussing whether he should come home to recover before trying to get a job. They discussed the potential need for rehab or at least some therapy. But Sam was twenty-one. He would be making his own decisions. They felt powerless, scared and a bit angry at their son.

Aaron was allowed to graduate and walk for his diploma that summer, as long as he submitted a paper to one professor within four weeks of graduation. Aaron came through, but that meant that he extended his lease and would be staying in New York longer, at least through the end of the summer. Sam and Lynn gave him choices about coming home or finding a job if he wanted to stay in New York. He found a job selling phones at an AT&T store in the City. But jobs like that were temporary for Aaron. It only took a few months before he had left for "another opportunity". So since he graduated from college, Aaron had stayed up in New York as he went from job to job looking for what he called the "right fit". He hardly ever came home except for certain holidays. Sam and Lynn had become concerned about the distance between them and their eldest child. He recently had found a job in the marketing department of a technology "start-up". He said that he loved the people he was working with. Sam and Lynn would still occasionally send him money as gifts.

Conversations between Sam and Aaron over the last few years had often become tense since Sam always seemed to be lecturing his son about being more "grounded" and responsible. Aaron didn't appreciate the advice and avoided those calls with his father. Every time that Sam spoke to his son, he couldn't help but think about his brother. The similarities were too much for Sam not to worry that maybe a bit of Aaron's struggles were tied to genetics.

Sam blamed himself for being too hard on Aaron, but he was worried about him and his future. Sam recognized that he had not always been "present" for his kids when they needed him. He had given that job to their mother. He convinced himself that he was responsible for working, putting a roof over their heads and giving them the education that he thought they deserved to succeed. To do that, he had to work. So, he did, just like his father had done for him and his brother. But now Sam understood that all of that work had come with a price. He was still hoping he could fix it.

Aaron didn't think much about the impact on his family due to the life he had chosen. It was his life to live. Aaron just wanted to find his own happiness. From Aaron's perspective he realized that his parents loved him and wanted what was best for him, but he wasn't sure that they really understood him. He didn't want to be lectured to all the time, and he didn't want to feel as if he was disappointing them, so the less time he spent around them was actually easier for Aaron. He felt bad, but he felt that he had to figure his life out on his own.

Chapter 18

WHEN MAX'S BROTHER Jacob turned eighteen in October of 1941, he had enlisted in the Army. All the talk in their neighborhood was about Hitler killing the Jews in Europe. Jacob told his mother he would "kill Hitler himself" if he had the chance. Max's family was therefore more accepting of Max's decision to enlist because his older brother Jacob had already opened the door to fighting in the war. So, when Max turned eighteen in September of 1943, he joined the Navy. After basic training and some time on a merchant vessel carrying supplies to Europe, he asked to be transferred. He hoped to be placed on a warship. He was not completely clear about where he would be sent, but Max was willing to fight in the Atlantic or Pacific campaigns. The world was at war. The United States was fighting both Germany and Japan. Both enemies needed to be defeated.

Max sat in the mess hall. The coffee was bitter. He thought about his older brother Jacob. The D-Day invasion had taken place eight months before, in June 1944. Max wondered where Jacob was now. He envisioned him either in Paris saving the French or in Berlin capturing Hitler. The war in Europe was succeeding at a faster pace than they were in the Pacific. Max wondered if his brother was okay.

Max also thought about his mother. Max's father had passed away before the war had even started. She had two sons fighting in the war with little ability to know if they were alive or dead. He tried to imagine how hard that must be for her: simultaneously so proud that her boys were fighting for peace and their country and so worried that neither would come home. She was alone. She needed her sons to return home safely.

Chapter 19

FRIDAY HAD BEEN a packed day for Sam, full of meetings and phone calls. He was working with one team of associates on drafting jury charges and another team on preparing preliminary evidentiary motions. He was not at his desk when the call came through and didn't see the message until late afternoon. It was from his doctor's office. Typically, they would leave a message on his phone with the results of his lab tests on his phone, maybe with a comment like "If you have any questions, please call the doctor."

But this time was different. The message said: "the doctor would like to speak with you in person." They wanted him to call the doctor's office to schedule an appointment. Sam immediately thought the worst, his pulse quickening as he listened to the message again.

What had they found? When he'd been in for his annual physical the week before, it had seemed to go well. He had taken multiple regular blood tests, a heart scan, and a chest x-ray. His internist, Steve Davis, was an old friend whom Sam had gone to for years. Steve had said everything looked "fine." But now Sam worried. His mind raced. He accepted the fact that he was a little neurotic about life. He immediately thought of a scene in a Woody Allen movie he once saw where the character has a headache but convinced himself that he had a brain tumor.

But all Sam could think about was how bad the timing was. One more thing to add to Sam's ever-growing list of things to do or worry about.

He called the office and got an appointment for ten a.m. on

Monday. Then Sam hung up and wondered what he should do. Should he text Steve? Call him to find out what was happening? He had his cell number.

He looked at his phone for a moment and then figured that if it were really that bad, Steve would have called him directly. He tried not to worry. But he knew that he would be worried all weekend.

When he got home that night, he didn't say anything to Lynn but recognized that he was quieter than usual. He had nothing to say. There was probably nothing wrong, he repeated to himself. There was no reason to upset her. He didn't even know what it was. "She has enough on her plate," he rationalized. They watched some TV after dinner until Sam excused himself to go to bed early. "It's been a long day," he said.

She understood. Lynn didn't offer a rebuttal except to say, "I'll be upstairs soon."

As Sam climbed the stairs, he wondered to himself about his mortality. Even if the news turned out to be nothing, it was just another one of those wake-up calls to remind him that he would not live forever. Sam sometimes thought about the song "Dust in the Wind" by Kansas and the lyrics "We're just a drop of water in an endless sea" and "All your money won't another minute buy." Those words haunted Sam. Even so, as he trudged up the stairs, his thoughts turned to the work ahead of him Sunday for the upcoming trial and several other cases. He walked into the bathroom, turned on the sink, and splashed water on his face. He tried not to let the worry shake him. "Life is life," he repeated to himself. He stared at his aging face in the mirror. He looked into his own eyes in the reflection.

Sam felt old.

Chapter 20

I T HAD ALREADY been over a month since the assault on Iwo Jima had begun. As he had done every day since the start of the attack, Max tracked the planes as they left the flight deck of the Bunker Hill on his radar screen.

Max remained vigilant during the regular missions flown by the airman on the ship. Dozens of planes took off and landed as they continued to provide air support for the Marine push through the island. Again and again, Max had been told that if the Allies could take Iwo Jima, it would provide them a base that they could use to support more bombing flights over Tokyo. He was told time and again that if the Allies could take Iwo Jima, it would be the "beginning of the end" for the war.

The Japanese fighters or "Zeros" continued to challenge the ships that surrounded the island. The enemy planes would regularly appear out of the clouds embarking on strafing runs, overwhelming the surrounding ships with bullets. Men would duck for cover as the planes flew by. The Allied fighters would engage these planes in mid-air and the sailors would watch, mesmerized as the planes danced in the skies chasing each other until one of them would fall in defeat.

This time the planes arrived while Max was on the flight deck taking a break. The sounds of the bullets hitting against the deck and the armor plates of the flight tower rang loudly and echoed across the ship. As he hid in a stairwell waiting for the planes to pass, he realized that two pilots, waiting to take off from the deck, were injured by shrapnel that had penetrated the aircraft. As the plane leaked fuel, Max and others ran to the plane to help get the men out of their seats. Then they carried the two men below deck to the medical bay. After he laid the men on the awaiting gurneys, Max realized that his hands were soaked in blood and there was a stench that he felt in his nostrils. It was the combination of blood, gunpowder and the fuel. He would smell it for days.

Chapter 21

SAM AND LUCY opened the side door to Max's house on Sunday morning. "Dad, we're here," Sam called out as they came in.

Sam was still hoping to find the side door locked, but it had stayed open.

They had picked up some coffee and bagels along the way. They both knew it might be a long day.

As Sam put the hot coffee cups on the counter, he again thanked Lucy for helping him.

"Dad, don't worry. This is fine. I'm done for the semester. This will be a great way to spend time with you and Grandpa." His daughter smiled.

Sam smiled back. "Dad! We're here," he called out again to his father.

Since his dad lived alone, Sam always felt a bit of trepidation until he responded. Occasionally, he had images of his dad peacefully passing away under tucked sheets in his bed. Other times, he expected to see him somewhere on the floor, having fallen and unable to get help. He couldn't avoid either image flashing in his brain.

When he heard his dad answer, "In the basement," Sam exhaled.

When Sam and Lucy reached the bottom step of the partially finished basement, Lucy hung her arms around her grandfather and gave him a long steady hug.

"Lucy! So wonderful to see you." Max said.

"You too, Grandpa." She said as she released him from her grip.

"Another good semester?"

"Yes. Great. I won't know my grades for a while, but I'm halfway done. Only one more year."

"I'll try to stick around to be your first patient."

"Grandpa!" Lucy said as if she had tried to explain it to him a thousand times before. "I'll be working with kids, not grown-ups."

"I'm still a kid at heart," her grandfather said, chuckling as if he was performing for her.

Lucy smiled. Max smiled back at his granddaughter.

"Talking about kids," Max looked at his son. "Your mother kept everything belonging to the two of you down here. Boxes everywhere. Over there is your work from middle school!"

Sam laughed. "You're kidding me, really?" and walked over to the boxes stacked in the corner. He lifted the lid and flipped through the contents. Trophies, pictures, and school reports. This was Ben's box. A wave of sadness swept over Sam. His brother's life. In a box. He replaced the cardboard top and moved on to the box below. Opening it, his memories flashed to his awkward years in middle school. "Oh, someone, please give me a match!" he gasped.

"What is it, Dad?" Lucy asked.

As she stepped closer, he lifted a school picture from the box to show her a framed eight-by-eleven. It was the worst picture she had ever seen of him.

"Oh, my God," she exclaimed, laughing.

"Yeah, yeah," her father said defensively. "As if you never went through an awkward stage!"

"Has Mom seen this?"

"Maybe not. But lucky for me, there is a statute of limitations on annulments."

"I absolutely need to bring this home!" She grabbed the picture from him.

"Thanks, Dad," Sam said to his father sarcastically.

His father, sitting on an old couch in the finished part of the basement, said, "Don't blame me; blame your mother for keeping all of this." Then he added, "If you are going to make me move, then you're going to have to deal with these boxes. Everything down here is either yours or Ben's."

Sam looked around at what his mother had stored of her children's lives over the last fifty years. There was a lot. Even if he wanted to go through his own stuff, he had no idea what to do with Ben's. His brother had no children to share the memories with. The only person who really even knew him anymore was Sam. Sam wasn't sure what to do with the memories already stuck in his head about his older brother. He certainly didn't have room to add more.

"I'll get everything out, Dad. Don't worry. I'll handle the basement. I need you to concentrate on what you want to move to your apartment. Otherwise, I'm getting a company to come out and sell off the furniture."

His father sat on the couch, looking at one of the walls. A blank stare. He had spent his whole life accumulating things—just stuff. "You decorate your house," he said, "adorn the walls, fill up the closets. And then, one day, you just give it all away or sell what you can. I've lived in this house for over fifty years, Sam. I can't believe it's time to leave."

Sam didn't respond. He only continued to pack up the boxes and left his father's statement unanswered.

After a few moments Sam suggested they move back upstairs to "tackle the kitchen".

As they slowly climbed the stairs back to the kitchen Sam asked what his dad wanted to do with the extra dishes and silverware.

Max turned to his granddaughter. "Lucy. Takes what you want. One day you'll have your own house," Max said.

Lucy stared at her father who nodded his head in agreement and then she turned back to her grandfather. "Okay. Grandpa. So long as Mom and Dad will store it for me." She laughed. Max smiled at the response.

Later that afternoon, Lynn arrived with take-out Chinese food. Some of Dad's favorites: won ton soup and General Tso's chicken. Like the deli stuff, Sam knew that none of this was good for his dad, but he was always so happy when they brought it. And he had made it to ninety; surely, he was entitled to some fun. "No diets at ninety," Sam would say to his father.

As they sat around the kitchen table, Max asked Lucy about school and her social life. "So, any boys your parents aren't telling me about?"

"Grandpa…you're too funny," Lucy responded.

"I know I've told you this story a hundred times, but when I first saw your grandmother, I knew…"

"Dad," Sam interrupted, "these days, the kids don't even talk to each other. It's all on their phones and dating apps."

"Nonsense," Max countered. Then he looked at his granddaughter. "When you see a nice boy, make sure you say hello. He'll take it from there."

Sam looked at Lynn and smiled.

Max then asked, "How's your brother?"

Lucy struggled to answer her grandfather. She turned helplessly to her mother.

"Aaron's busy with work," Lynn interrupted. As she stood to start clearing the dishes, she added, "He's going to be thirty soon! It's about time he finds a nice girl." Her tone was serious.

Max looked at Sam. Sam just shrugged.

"Let me help you with those dishes," Max said, rising from his chair—but just as quickly, he dropped back down, almost tumbling off. Sam saw it happen and grabbed his father's shoulder before he hit the ground. Although his father had always been a big, strong man, as the years passed, he had begun to diminish.

Sam was able to grab his dad's shoulder and straighten him on the chair in time to avoid a fall. "What was that Dad?" he asked, catching his breath from the surprise.

"Just lost my balance, son. Good catch." Max's eyes were still wide from the increased blood pumping through his startled heart.

"You sure you're okay?" Sam asked.

"Fine," his dad said. He was embarrassed. "Not a scratch. All fine." He found his composure and added, "Thanks for dinner. I'm going to bed." This time he stood, solidly grabbed his walker, and began his march down the hall. "Goodnight, all," he said without turning around. "I'll let you close up."

Lucy followed her grandfather down the hall, stopped him, and hugged him. "Goodnight, Grandpa," she said.

Sam looked at his wife with sadness in his expression. They both had seen the sweetness of the moment, but there was nothing they could say.

His dad was getting old; Sam knew that. He was rational about it. But he was trying to balance his concern about his father's dignity against Sam's fear that his father could not care for himself. Sam recognized that he was the child becoming the parent. The circle of life. And there was Max with his granddaughter. One day, Lucy would take care of Sam and Lynn just as they tried to care for his father. Where did the time go?

Lynn finished cleaning the kitchen with Lucy. As they turned to leave, Sam looked around his old house. So many memories of his time growing up in Nashville. He thought to himself how simpler those times seemed to be. Back then, Sam had no worries. How things had changed.

Chapter 22

THE SHIP STEADILY remained on high alert through the battle over Iwo Jima. The Allied forces were making progress, but success came at a high cost. Max heard the reports of mortar shells and machine gun fire raining down on the Marines from the mountain ranges controlled by the Japanese.

But as the Marines kept pushing, men replaced men. Troop ships guarded by destroyers delivered thousands. Some were seasoned soldiers, having battled through Guadalcanal, Guam, and the Marianas. Some were fresh from basic training. They had no idea what faced them. The reports had been horrible. Max listened from the CIC. Although the Allies were making ground, thousands were being wounded and killed.

During their breaks, the men would meet in the mess hall to play cards. Max had just left the CIC and entered the mess hall. He grabbed a cup of coffee and sat at the table with his crew mates.

"Five card stud, jacks wild," Tony said and then he dished out the cards to the five men in the circle around him.

Max looked at the first two cards that had been dealt down to him, shielding his prize from the wandering eyes of his bunkmates. He held a jack and a seven. Tony pointed to Ryan on his left. "Bet?" he asked.

Ryan placed down a cigarette as a bet. Tony turned to each player until he got to Max. Each player "called" and dropped a cigarette on the table.

Max smiled as he said, "Raise it," and placed two cigarettes in front of him, ecstatic that he was already holding a wild card.

The other guys mouthed off about his bet, and a chorus of "Fold" spread around the table. Tony looked at his friend and said, "You scared them off, but not me," dropping two cigarettes on the table.

Max laughed.

Tony issued the three remaining cards to Max and said, "Your bet, buddy."

Max pulled the cards from the table. He had been given a king, a two and another seven. Max looked at Tony and said, "Check," not wanting to sucker his friend into a large bet but also wondering what Tony would do with his cards.

Tony placed five cigarettes on the table. "So, buddy. Call or raise? Or do you fold?" Tony winked at his friend as if he was holding four jacks in his hand.

Max was about to answer when the general alarm sounded. The men at the table jumped from their seats, grabbed their vests, and started to move from the bunk. Tony and Max looked at each other and said, "We'll finish this later." Quickly, they divided the cigarettes on the table, each taking a handful.

"Shoot 'em straight," Max said to his friend.

"Make sure you let me know where they are coming from, Mr. Radarman," Tony replied. Tony slapped his buddy on the shoulders and said, "Stay safe," as he exited for the upper deck and Max headed below deck to the CIC.

With pure instinct, Max threw his life vest around his shoulders as he made his way down the metal stairs into the belly of the ship towards the Radar room. The life vest was so bulky that he knew he could not wear it in the CIC. But there was always the risk that the ship would be hit, the water would come, and he would need it. But as he turned back down another level of stairs to the CIC, he also realized it wouldn't matter. If the ship were to sink, he would never be able to swim out. There would be no need for the vest.

Chapter 23

WHEN SAM AND Lynn first moved to New York after Sam graduated from law school, they lived in a small one-bedroom apartment on the Upper West Side, but when Aaron was born, it didn't take them long to decide to head to Westchester to a house with a backyard where he could play. Lucy was born three years later. Sam took the train to the office every day and most weekends, or he worked at home at night in a study they had built off the first-floor living room.

As the kids got older and work grew more intense there were plenty of times that Sam and Lynn talked about moving back to Nashville. The thought tormented him as he balanced his professional success with his job's impact on the kids and his relationship with Lynn. She had accepted that work was his top priority even though Sam never admitted it. They would argue over missed parent-teacher meetings or other activities because Sam had somehow convinced himself that if he worked, he was "doing it for them."

When his dad turned eighty, it had been a trigger point for Sam. His mom had cancer. His parents needed help even though they said they didn't. Even though Ben lived in the same town as his parents, he was useless, so Sam would inevitably find himself flying back and forth to Nashville to help his aging parents as they spent more and more time with doctors.

At that time the conversations went back and forth more often about whether Sam and his family would leave New York. The talks became more sincere. It would mean less pay, but he also knew that if he didn't leave now, he never would.

He thought he would somehow be making amends if he moved back after being away for twenty years—that by moving back now, he could somehow make up for the time that he had been away, living his own life.

Once he decided to look around Nashville for jobs, he contacted a recruiter. It wasn't long before Taylor & Burton, a large Nashville firm, offered him a great job running the firm's litigation team. He came well qualified after his work in New York and, thankfully, had kept his Tennessee license active all these years just for this possibility. At least for work, it would be a relatively easy transition.

Lynn understood Sam's feelings about moving back. She had been ready to move back since they had gotten to New York. She accepted that they had moved there for the better job, the money, and the spoils that came with it, but she did not love living in New York. She felt constant pressure to keep up with the "Joneses" and was certain the kids felt the same way around their friends. Plus, she missed her family. She had returned home to Knoxville as much as possible to see her aging parents and spend time with her siblings, all of whom still lived there, but it was not the same. She said yes to the move as soon as Sam mentioned the job offer.

The timing was good for Lucy since she would be starting high school, and they assumed there would be a minimal impact on Aaron since he would be leaving that fall for college.

They started shopping for a house in Nashville. It would be more house than they could have ever afforded in New York, and Sam would lose the train commute.

Sam was convinced it was the right time for all of them. He was glad that he could be close to his parents again. He had been away from them for too long. They needed him, and in many ways, he needed them.

Chapter 24

THE BUNKER HILL was heavily equipped with both offensive and defensive weaponry. Some of the guns were massive and the ship held over a dozen anti-aircraft canons. Tony was a gun captain for one of the forty-millimeter cannons mounted next to the flight control tower. Each turret had space for six men. The canons extended from each turret from about eight to ten feet. The turrets moved up and down and side to side to track the enemy aircraft. Without these guns, the carrier would have been a defenseless target, just a floating football field for target practice to the enemy.

Tony climbed into his gun turret and took hold of the five-inch, eighty caliber- cannon. The weapon fired one hundred and sixty rounds per minute per barrel, each with a range of four thousand yards.

Max was working in the CIC when the planes arrived. He saw the enemy aircraft on his radar screen as they approached from the north. The alarms were sounded.

On deck, Tony positioned his gun to fire in anticipation of the fast-traveling Zero that had reduced its altitude and readied itself for an approach. The team of six assigned to the gun worked in unison to replace the ammunition as Tony, the "gun captain," directed the angle and movement of the weapon to intersect the plane's approach. Smoke emanated from the canon each time it fired, blackening the air around them as they continued to defend the ship. One of Tony's shipmates yelled, "Drop that asshole!" as he loaded another round of ammunition into the armament. Each explosion rocked the team that surrounded the weapon, but they remained steady in their focus. The same symmetry of moving "ammunition to gun" was happening around the ship as each munitions team in each of of the separate turrets around the ship focused on the most aggressive approaching aircraft.

Tony joined the other sailors in their respective turrets to respond to the enemy aircraft as they attacked the carrier and the other ships that surrounded the island. Shells blasted as the sailors targeted the planes, advancing their scopes to anticipate their altitude and acceleration. The skies grew dark as the gunpowder from the shells exploded against the targeted planes, puffs of black smoke filling the air above the ship.

Crew members watched and cheered as Tony hit the wing of the first plane and scored a direct hit on the other. Both planes were spinning as they sailed toward the water with smoke and fire trailing behind them. Each plane splashed and exploded upon impact.

When he was done, Tony had successfully downed the two zeros. Grabbing a spent bullet, he scratched two more marks on the turret. He held the record on the ship.

In the CIC, peace came over the group after the last bogie had been splashed, and no other planes appeared on the radar. Everyone knew that this was a temporary reprieve; there would be more coming. These daily battles had diminished the Japanese Imperial Air Service, but they were manufacturing new planes and recruiting new pilots every day. The Japanese pilots were getting younger and younger, many being sent to fly these missions with no experience and no ability to evade the Allies' anti-aircraft weaponry.

The attack on Pearl Harbor had been a rallying cry for the United States. The Country had never been attacked before like that. The United States would not stop its pursuit of Japan until it made its country safe again. Many sailors wondered how Japan could sacrifice so many citizens for this war and why the country continued to pursue this effort at conquest.

Chapter 25

A S SAM, LYNN, and Lucy drove home from his Max's house Sunday night, Sam kept thinking about his father falling from his chair. He knew that they had made the right decision to move him into the center. As he drove home, he reminded himself of the tour of the "senior living" facility he'd taken with Lynn and his dad a few months before. They had signed the paperwork for his apartment even though Max had not yet agreed to move.

When they toured the center, both Sam and Lynn were pleased to see the list of social activities offered at the facility each day. "Plenty to keep you busy," they reminded Max as they walked the hallways.

Sam's father had not been amused. From his perspective, he was being asked, or essentially told, to leave his good-sized home, where he had lived for more than fifty years, for a one-bedroom apartment, where he would be expected to spend his days participating in bingo games and sing-a-longs. Max still saw himself as independent and capable. He was being told to move to a place where he would be seen as weak and potentially incompetent.

"This is hell," he had said to his son and daughter-in-law. "I'm not going to do it."

Sam had ignored the comment. He certainly could understand his dad's hesitation, but he had talked to Lynn about this. They discussed that Max's condition was slowly declining, and they were constantly worried about his living in the house alone. It was inevitable that he would have to move to someplace smaller and get some everyday help, maybe even nursing. The stress of worrying about him kept them up at night.

"You can always just move in with us," Sam reminded his dad of the offer he and Lynn had made multiple times. "The kids are gone. We're empty nesters!" they would say. They had enough room in the house to offer Max his own space and privacy. But Max saw the invitation as a similar example of his perceived failures. From his perspective, he would move in and be treated like a child while still seeing himself as the parent. Max just could not come to terms with how his own family perceived him. He saw himself differently. He was a bit angry and clearly defensive about the whole ordeal.

Sam reflected on the conversation they had after the tour. "Dad, just think about it. We can come back another time to visit again." But Sam knew that his dad was not happy, and Sam felt awful. The drive back to his house after the tour had been quiet. It was clear that everyone in the car was deep in their own thoughts. Max had just stared out the window. He was thinking about Rose. How his life had been. He couldn't believe he was visiting retirement homes. His eyes only saw the youth of his life. But he was beginning to see that he wasn't the same person anymore.

When Sam and Lynn got home that night, they didn't mention another word about what happened to Max until they both had gotten into bed.

"He's getting weaker," she said.

"I know. I know."

"It's the right time for him to move. It will be safer at the center," she added. Then she said to her husband, "It is a nice place."

Sam smiled and answered, "Feel free to move me in now. I love bingo!"

Lynn countered, "I put in our reservation. I'll play mahjong all day, and I won't have to cook again!"

"So, Dad can just take our house, and we'll be fine there," Sam smiled. They both laughed.

"We're living life as the 'sandwich generation,'" Sam said to his wife. "Our parents are living longer. We're taking care of them and our kids at the same time."

"True, but a good problem to have, right? Living longer, that is. Applies to us, too, right?" she asked.

"Do you think the kids will care for us the same way we care for our parents?" Lynn asked Sam.

"Aaron told me once that he'll pull the plug on us right now if we wanted to." he said with a laugh, adding, "I may take him up on that."

Sam let out a long breath. He closed his eyes.

"I'm exhausted. Always balancing the plates, riding the unicycle, dodging the balls."

"Circus metaphors?" she asked.

"Just life, I guess." Sam responded.

"We're lucky that your dad is still a part of our lives. We have to feel good about that." Lynn said as she up on pulled the covers.

"I know, but there's no instruction book for any of this. Managing all of the pieces, how they all fit, where they are supposed to go."

Lynn didn't respond. She rolled over and said "but consider the alternative."

"Fake it till you make it. Isn't that the road map for life anyway?" he said, more to himself than to her. "Man plans, God laughs."

Sam felt the tension about his dad. But he was also at a loss for how to handle the situation. Of course, he loved his dad and wanted to protect him. Leaving him to decline alone in the house and worry about him all the time just wasn't right. He saw the situation from the perspective of the child. The effort to take care of the parent. He wasn't thinking about any of it from his dad's perspective. He didn't realize how hard this must be for him.

Sam maybe understood some of this based on what had happened with his mom. She had tried to reject her last chemotherapy session, pleading that she had had "enough." She just wanted to have some quality of life before her time came. The constant doctor visits and medications had exhausted her, and she experienced severe side effects from the treatments, including difficult abdominal pain. But

Sam kept pushing back, pleading with her to fight more and continue her treatment.

After she was gone, Sam realized that he wanted her to keep fighting for her life only because he didn't want to lose her. He was thinking about himself. He never really thought about what she felt or needed. He didn't want to suffer her loss. And it was happening again. Sam wanted his dad to move into the center because he knew it would make him feel better. He really wasn't giving his father the credit he deserved to decide what he wanted for himself.

But Sam was just doing what he understood society expected of him. It seemed like everyone Sam knew who had elderly parents were moving them into nursing homes or "independent living centers." No one seemed to be able to live on their own. Sam wanted to protect his father. But his father just wanted to live his own life. He wanted to stay in the home he had lived and shared with his wife for over fifty years. Sam understood that his father just wanted dignity and independence. Sam couldn't blame his dad when he complained about the center. Sam felt like he was putting his father into prison and taking away his freedom. Sam understood, he internally recognized, that if you lived to a certain age, you would inevitably have to accept help. Sam felt like there were no other choices now. The center seemed to be the only solution for his dad.

Sam turned off the lights and softly settled into his side of the bed. Sam understood the emotion of all of this took its toll. He had always idolized his dad. He'd always seemed unbeatable, but it was becoming clear that, like his mom, his dad was going to eventually lose this battle. Life was creeping up on his dad. Sam thought that "life is short, especially when you're ninety."

Chapter 26

A S EACH DAY passed, Max watched the battle continue. If he wasn't sitting in the CIC, he was back on the flight deck watching the explosions and air assaults on the island. With every bomb or rocket that exploded, he imagined the worst happening on the island. He thought he could feel men being killed. He internalized the fear of death for the men, some of whom were younger than him. He was relieved to be on the ship. He felt safer, at least for now. But he felt guilty that he wasn't one of the soldiers fighting on the island.

There was little reprieve for either side. Over time, being short on water, food, and supplies, the Japanese became desperate in their attacks. Rumors of the massacres on the American forces were horrific. It was clear that thousands were dead, and many more had been wounded. Balanced against the American losses, Max heard estimates that over twenty-thousand Japanese soldiers had been killed during the few weeks of fighting.

There were nights when Max would lie on his bunk for hours, unable to sleep. Even though he was exhausted, all he could think about were the soldiers who were dying. He was trying to understand what was happening. How did it come to be that Hitler wanted to control Europe and the Japanese the Pacific? How many millions would have to die following dictators and emperors who craved power?

As the days wore on, eventually, the Japanese would be overcome by the unceasing barrage of ground forces that landed on Iwo Jima. After five weeks, platoons of Japanese soldiers started to surrender. Troops raised the American flag on Mount Suribachi on February 23, 1945.

Chapter 27

LYNN HAD BEEN a member of the Silver family for over three decades, so she had earned a front-row seat to the dynamics of what it meant to be a "Silver." Over the last ten years, she had witnessed Rose coming to terms with her cancer, Max losing his wife, and Sam losing his mother and brother.

Her brother-in-law Ben had been a topic at her in-laws' dinner table since she and Sam had married. The stories had sometimes been troubling to hear. His life was often a mess. So, Lynn understood why Sam was worried about Aaron. He was worried that the same thing could happen to Aaron. Sam had also watched how Ben's troubles had alienated Ben from his parents. Sam didn't want that to happen with his family.

It was no surprise to Lynn that after Aaron graduated from college, he chose to stay in New York. He had learned from his own family that it was okay to move away and live your own life. Certainly, Aaron would not understand what being away may have meant for his parents, how they longed to stay connected and felt distant from the children they had raised. Sam had understood that only after he had returned to Nashville. It would be a while before Aaron could understand what Sam was feeling.

Lynn understood how much it hurt Sam to be separated from his son and to sense that Aaron didn't seem to need him anymore. Lynn believed that may have been one of the reasons that Sam was so concerned about his dad. Sam needed to be needed. He felt responsible for everyone around him.

Lynn knew Sam sometimes better than he knew himself. It wasn't easy to convince Sam that she knew best, but she could only remember a few times he failed to give way to her.

Rose was like Sam. She had worked to fix everyone and everything in her family. Lynn could remember times when Rose tried to influence what Sam was doing and, even more so, how they were raising the kids in New York. Sam didn't like the conflict his mother sometimes created, but Lynn understood that Rose was only trying to help. She was a mother. Lynn scoffed at Sam's stereotype of a "Jewish" mother since she was convinced that all mothers tended to interfere in their children's lives.

There were certainly a few times when Lynn and Rose had clashed over things, but again, Max and Rose lived in Nashville, and Sam and Lynn only visited a few times a year. Sam and Lynn were leading separate lives most of the time in New York.

It was different when Sam and Lynn moved back. Rose was sick and Lynn acted like a nurse for her. They grew very close over those last years they were together. Rose had lost whatever edge she may have had for Lynn by that time. Sam and Lynn had already been married over twenty years and had raised two children. Her grandchildren. And they were stable as a family. Rose saw a lot of herself in Lynn. Rose knew that Lynn understood what it meant to raise a family.

As a gift to Rose, Lynn finally went through the process of conversion to be Jewish. Lynn and Sam joined his parent's synagogue, Temple Shalom, and Lynn studied for months, meeting with the rabbi, reading books and practicing her readings. The whole family was together at the ceremony. Max read from the Torah. It had made Rose very happy to see her daughter-in-law convert. Rose told Aaron and Lucy after the ceremony how important it was that they find someone who would carry on their faith.

Rose and Lynn grew closer every day, especially in the last few days of Rose's life. Rose passed away only three months after Lynn's conversion.

Chapter 28

A FTER THE FLAG was raised on Mount Suribachi, it took almost another month for the Allies to fully secure the island.

After the battles subsided on Iwo Jima, there was a relaxation of the tension that permeated the crew of the Bunker Hill. As the ship readied itself to move to its next target, everything became somewhat normal again. It was evident in how they talked, smoked cigarettes, and everything else. They were, however, still on guard: With just one indication of an unidentified plane or ship, they would have reverted to the efficient plotters, operators, fighter directors, and monitors that they were.

Even with this victory, Max understood that the Japanese were not giving up.

The Bunker Hill set its sights for the island of Okinawa. Everyone knew that Okinawa was a final piece of Japan's defense. The Japanese would do everything they could to stop the Americans from succeeding. Although he had hoped and even prayed for it to be over, Max knew the war was still far from ending.

As they approached the island, the skies were again filled with enemy planes. Each dogfight between aircraft resulted in the risk of pilot loss. Each victory was replaced by another threat. The men showed no fear, but each wondered when the barrage of gunfire would end and whether they would be alive to see it.

Chapter 29

S AM THOUGHT ABOUT Aaron. He missed him. Sam believed that much of their distance was because he worked too often and wasn't home as much as he should have been. He had been very busy with his practice when he first got started. Long hours in the office. Few hours at home. Weekends at his desk, even if he had little to do. It's what was expected when you were working your way up the ladder. Facetime with the partners, who would also occasionally appear in the office after their mornings at the country club. But young associates thought they understood how the game was played. Work the hours, build up the credit, and then you would make partner as well—the holy grail. You, too, would eventually make partner, maybe seven to twelve years down the road. You, too, would be dropping by the office to visit your minions of associates on the weekend. It was the cycle, and Sam had bought in. So had Lynn: He would work, and she would raise the kids.

So, while Sam hadn't been to every soccer or baseball game Aaron had played and hadn't been there to play catch in the yard, he was doing what was necessary to provide for his family.

He couldn't blame Aaron for doing the same thing with his life. He was allowed to live his own life. He didn't need to stay in Nashville. Sam just missed him. Sam thought that they were drifting apart, and he blamed himself. He had often been too busy at work or, after they moved back to Nashville, too preoccupied with helping his parents. He was feeling disconnected from his son. Sam felt that even when they had talked, their conversations had been rushed and superficial.

Soon after the family had moved to Nashville to be with Sam's parents, Aaron left for college. He didn't watch as his dad tried to reconnect with his own father to make up for lost time. He didn't see his dad struggle to make up for the lost years that they had drifted apart.

Sam felt like he was losing touch with Aaron as he grew up and moved on, but he understood that he had done the same thing when he left town after law school. Sam was very cognizant of Harry Chapin's "Cat's in the Cradle" theme that underscored the distance that he thought he had created with his son. The song played in his head.

"and as I hung up the phone, it occurred to me
He'd grown up just like me
My boy was just like me."

He sat in bed thinking about his circumstances. The weight of the world was on Sam. His mind was racing. He knew that he had his doctor's appointment in the morning. Sam was assuming that he would get bad news when he talked to Steve. He always expected the worst, even while hoping for the best. It was one of Sam's worst character flaws. He wished he could be more optimistic. He just found it hard to do, especially in the last few years.

He stared at the ceiling as Lynn slept peacefully. It would be a long night.

Chapter 30

THE MARINES BEGAN their assault on the island of Okinawa on April 1, 1945, only days after completing their occupation of Iwo Jima.

The Allied attack would be code-named "Operation Iceberg," one of the last pieces of the unified invasion plans for Japan and "Operation Downfall." The Allies had focused their armada on this remaining fortified island. Between the Army and Marines, the United States personnel who attacked the island consisted of more than 180,000 men against 90,000 combined Japanese military and conscripted citizens of Okinawa.

As its defenses fell, the Imperial Japanese forces increased the intensity of air attacks against the ships operating off Okinawa. Although many Japanese pilots still released bombs that struck the targeted ships, the Americans began to witness a new threat in the waters off Okinawa. In desperation against the approaching American threat, the Japanese began to recruit kamikaze pilots who agreed to sacrifice their lives for their homeland. Five days after the initial landing on Okinawa, a wave of more than 300 Japanese aircraft struck the armada of Allied ships supporting the attack. This offensive on April 6, 1945, would be known as "Operation Ten-Go." Planes were everywhere. Guns blasted from the decks of the battleships and carriers to challenge the aircraft as they aimed directly for the heart of the ships. Smoke filled the air as the battle raged on. Those Japanese fighters who missed their mark finished as demolished instruments of death floating in the East China Sea.

Max understood that the carriers' flight decks were the largest targets among the floating warships. He remained on high alert, as did the entire crew.

Max, Tony, and Ryan would meet on deck or in the mess hall when they took their breaks. They were all killing time until the next assault. They shared news from their families and rumors about the war. They had been at sea for more than three months, and the ship smelled of sea air and sweat. The coffee had grown weaker, and the men's spirits were dampened by the days of fighting that seemed endless. They laughed when they could and promised each other visits to their homes back in the States after the war ended. They all hoped to keep their promises.

Chapter 31

MONDAY'S APPOINTMENT COULD not have come soon enough for Sam. As the nurse softly closed the door behind him, he walked into the exam room. She had said the doctor would be with him in a minute, but Sam knew that wasn't true. He had already been waiting fifteen minutes past his scheduled appointment in the waiting room. But that wasn't unusual. Patients were always waiting to see their doctors. That's why it's called a waiting room. Sam smiled and shook his head. He never made his clients wait. When his clients arrived at his firm, they were ceremoniously asked to wait in the reception area to lounge on coffee and refreshments while he would travel from his office and welcome them there. What a difference. But Sam chuckled that patients would wait to see their doctor because their lives depended on it. Lawyers, well, they were just lawyers.

Dr. Steven Davis knocked gently on the door before opening it and extended his hand to Sam. "Sam, thanks for coming in. Good to see you."

"I wish I could say the same," Sam responded, smiling. He had just been in the office last week. There was no small talk left for them.

"Steve. What's this about? What's the problem?"

"Okay," the doctor said as he grabbed a wheeled stool that was across the room and rolled himself with his feet like a children's toy until he reached his patient. "We got your test results. You have an unusually high PSA. There are some other indicators in your tests that show an issue."

"Like the fact that I have to piss all the time?" Sam tried to joke away his tension. It was his prostate. His father had had prostate cancer in his seventies.

"It's really high," his doctor replied. "We sent the file to a urologist specializing in oncology. I wanted to be able to answer your questions in person. I didn't want to do this over the phone. Eventually, you'll have to see this other doctor."

Sam sat quietly. He was somewhat relieved. He understood what it meant to have this condition. He was of a certain age, and it was not uncommon. He was scared, but not as scared as he would have been had it been something else. This didn't seem as foreign. His dad had lived through it, as had some of his friends.

The doctor explained the test results but clarified that a biopsy would be needed to confirm his findings. "If it is what I think, then we caught it early," his doctor repeated.

Sam took a deep breath. He wasn't going to show his emotions in front of his friend. That was for another time and place. He didn't want to make his friend uncomfortable. So, Sam just said, "I'm good, Steve," reaching out his hand. "Thanks for calling me in. I'll follow up with the other doctor. I will."

"I'm sorry I had to be the one to tell you," Steve said as they shook hands.

Sam left the doctor's office and slowly walked to his car in the adjacent parking garage. When he found his car, he got into the driver's seat but failed to press the ignition button. Instead, he just sat there for a moment, soaking up the realization that he was sixty and time was starting to catch up with him.

He always knew that he would not escape life without something like this happening. He wasn't bulletproof. He had tried to stay healthy all these years, but he blamed the stress. As crazy as it was, he had blamed his mother's stress over the years about Ben for her eventual cancer.

"The worrying catches up with you," he would think. He knew that if he continued to stress himself, it would eventually catch up with him, too. He figured it finally had.

Sam had known something was wrong the past few months. It was his body telling him that something was wrong. He had attributed it to his anxieties at work, but he wasn't surprised to learn that it was something else. He was sixty, a time when things started, inevitably, to break down. It had been his knees first from running. Then his shoulder from playing golf, and now this. He had watched his dad, his model of what a man should be, begin to decay as he hit seventy. The body was just "a rental," his dad would say. Sam was just starting to understand the meaning of his words.

But as he sat in the car, he tried to put his new medical news into perspective. It was "early," Steve had said. He would be okay. It would be just another of those battles in life his dad always talked about. He knew he would be fine; at the same time, this came at such a crazy time for him. He thought about everything at work, home, with his dad—and even their upcoming trip.

On the drive home, Sam kept thinking about life's warning signs. He had just gotten another one. How many more would he get before he stopped to really appreciate his life? He promised himself that he would try to do better when he returned from the trip.

He also began to think about his faith. Would he pray that everything would be okay? Sam had grappled with his religion many times. His prayers had not been answered when his mom got sick. He had chastised God when Ben died. Over the last few years, Sam had questioned his need for religion when he did not clearly understand what his faith even meant to him.

Sam's connection to his religion had always been a struggle for him. It didn't get any easier when he met Lynn, but their different religions had not been an issue for Sam when they married. She had even agreed to raise the kids Jewish. But back then it was all a function of appearances. They were checking all the boxes to be part of their community in New York. At its core, Sam struggled to understand his relationship with God, any god. He had failed to find a connection to his religion to help him cope with the loss of his mother or his brother, and he was not confident that he would find the answer when it came to his own health. But he hoped he would. He knew that he would find himself asking for help from a higher power. He often found himself praying, he just wasn't sure who he was praying to. He knew that he needed to find the time and the commitment to rebuild his connection to his faith. There was no better time to do that than now. With everything going on he knew he would be needing the extra help.

As he thought about the possibility of a bad diagnosis, Sam knew he wouldn't say anything to anyone until he returned from the trip, especially his dad. It would only worry him, and there was nothing he could do anyway. There was no reason for him to know. He thought about Lynn too. She would be upset that he didn't tell her. But again, there was nothing she could do. He would deal with it when he returned from the weekend with his dad. Another few days wouldn't matter.

Chapter 32

ON APRIL 12, 1945, word spread around the ship that President Roosevelt had died. He had been their Commander in Chief. A four-term President. Both sadness and fear swept through the crew of the Bunker Hill about the loss of their leader. The timing concerned Max as they were suffering so many setbacks off Okinawa. Already, over twenty American ships had been lost to kamikaze attacks that month and over a hundred and fifty ships had been damaged. Max was worried about the desperate shifting strategy of the Japanese forces.

Max sat in the mess hall with his crew mates. They talked about Roosevelt like they would a father. He had led these men for over seven years as their President. He inspired them to go to war, to risk their lives as Americans. But they understood that he would not be alive to see the war end.

They toasted him "To FDR" with their coffee cups. Then they added. "Now on to Tokyo!".

Chapter 33

THE CAB HAD picked Max up at his house on Wednesday morning. The driver had promised that he would also stay to drive Max home. Max offered him a twenty-dollar tip for waiting for him during his visit.

"Wait right here," Max said to the driver, who had pulled Max's walker from the trunk of the car.

"You okay, sir?" the driver asked as Max steadied himself with his walker and turned toward the gravel walkway.

"Yes. Fine. It will be about fifteen minutes." Max explained to the driver again. He walked slowly down the path, his view fixed on the tombstones ahead. The Jewish cemetery was just a few miles from his house. He had made this trip every week for the past five years—a visit to see Rose.

Max and Rose were married ten days after he returned from the war. He still had bandages on his hands from his burns, but they held hands together under the chuppah as the Brooklyn rabbi blessed their marriage.

They initially lived with Rose's parents. Her father was a doctor, and her parents' suburban Connecticut house was large enough for the new couple to get settled and start their life. But Max would not be satisfied living under his in-laws' shadow. He wanted to make his own mark and provide for his future family.

They wanted children, many of them, but Rose had difficulty with the pregnancies. It took four years before Ben arrived, and later Sam's birth was a miracle to them. The brothers were a little more than five years apart, and between their births, there had been two other miscarriages.

After Ben was born, Max took a job as a salesman with a growing home-building company in New York. The travel was constant and draining, but Max was demonstrating his success in business.

After a year, Max was asked by his company to open a branch for them in Nashville Tennessee. It was 1950 and would be an exciting time to make such a change, as the post-war growth continued to fuel home sales. Max and Rose agreed that moving away from the Northeast would not be easy. It would be a challenging time for a Jewish family to start over in the South. They both understood that life would be different there. But after they talked about it, Max accepted the offer. He would oversee the company's home building expansion into the South.

Rose was still hesitant to leave her family and surroundings but recognized that Max wanted to carve out his own success in the world. She would support anything he wanted to do. They were in love. During the war, she was certain she would lose him. So many had died—but he had come home to her, and she would not risk losing him again. And so they left to find their lives in another community, as pioneers staking a claim.

They would raise their family in Nashville. They would make a life there. Once they arrived, they would never leave.

Two years later, Max left his job with the home building company and started a sales and distribution company selling building equipment. As he had hoped, the South continued to grow, and he built a successful company. Sam was born a few years later. Then they built the house that Max now was living in. Their family's house. He held his business together through economic ups and downs for over fifty years. His children did not want to take it over, so when Max retired at eighty, he sold it to employees who shared his passion and promised they would care for the company. His payout would allow Rose and him to travel and enjoy their retirement.

But then Rose got sick. Once that happened, they realized they had waited too long to do the traveling they had planned. They realized that their golden years would not be as golden as they were supposed to be.

As he walked the path toward Rose's headstone, Max's peripheral vision caught the familiar names of those buried in this section, an area reserved for his synagogue. He either knew the people when they were alive or had memorized the names as part of his weekly pilgrimage here.

As he came to the end of the path, he stopped and looked down. In front of him was the double tombstone created for Max and Rose. As he often did, he visually measured the square footage of the area below her name and the equal piece of earth waiting for him when the time came.

"Hi, honey," he said. "Busy week. Lots to tell you", he explained to the granite piece that adorned her name.

"Rose, I'm going to the reunion this year. I think it's time. Thank you for being patient." He spoke lovingly to his wife, telling her about his visit from Lucy and about his planned trip with Sam. Then, he touched his fingers to his lips and reached forward slowly with a shaking hand to place the kiss on the crown of her tombstone. As he steadied himself on the monument, he put his hand in his coat pocket, removed a small rounded, colorful stone, and dropped it at the base of the marker. It joined the dozens of other stones that had been placed there.

Max turned back toward the waiting cab but stopped in his tracks. He looked to his left. "Hey, Benny," he said out loud. "I miss you." He took a long, deep breath and filled his lungs with air. He felt the air inside of him as his chest expanded. When he exhaled, he released some of the stress that he felt. The sun was out. The trees moved slowly, almost rhythmically, with the wind. He took a moment. He was standing here. He was still alive, a walking, talking person. He felt somewhat awed by the fact that he had somehow survived, not just the war, but life itself, for ninety years. It was a pretty good run. He had seen a lot, done a lot. He had lived a good life. But he couldn't help but think about Rose. He had outlived her. He wasn't supposed to. He was supposed to go first. He had lived the last five years without her by his side. It was a miracle that he had made it this far.

That night Max tried to sleep. But he hadn't been sleeping very well. Instead, his brain regularly offered him images from his life that he hadn't seen in years. When he closed his eyes, photos of his life passed before him, each for a moment at a time. Some were good, and some were bad. He realized that he had locked away much of who he was and what he had experienced over the last seventy years since the war.

He thought he had done everything he could with the time God granted him on this earth. Maybe he could have done more. He had survived the losses, the challenges, and the disappointments. He had been lifted by the successes, the joys, and the love. Max thought of himself as practical. There was not much left for him to do.

He realized many of his thoughts were shaped by his energy ahead of the reunion. He was nervous about going, but he was excited as well. It was a part of his life that he had sequestered away. So much loss, so much sadness. But it was also the defining moment in his life. He wanted to return to that time to remember who he was. There would be others there as well. And ghosts, so many ghosts.

Chapter 34

A S THE CALENDAR turned to May, the flights off the deck of the Bunker Hill and the bombardment of Okinawa continued daily. Waves of planes left the ship to support the growing number of Marines that had landed on the island. Heavy rains impeded the advancement of the Americans, and the Japanese took advantage of their strategic defenses to maintain relentless counterattacks against the weary soldiers. As they had on Iwo Jima, the Japanese forces fought tenaciously against the Allied incursion.

That night Max wrote to Rose. His words were terse because each time the ship rattled, Max assumed the worse. He did not have much to say to her. His days had become a string of shifts in the CIC and breaks in the mess hall or on deck. Otherwise, he slept when he could. It was becoming monotonous. He had only been at sea since the end of January, but it felt like an eternity. He thought the war might never end. Another battle, another death, another ship, another shell, another explosion. He started a new cigarette as he finished the one before and drank the dank dark swill of the coffee served in the mess hall. He thought of home, walking through the streets of Brooklyn. Life was so easy there. He longed for home.

Chapter 35

I T WAS ALREADY Thursday. Sam and his dad were scheduled to leave the next morning. Over the last few days, Sam had done his best to delegate pieces of the class action case among his partners and associates. He had worked most of the day, furiously sending e-mails to his team assigning last-minute trial preparation. He had planned to do these tasks himself, but he was running out of time. "No bandwidth," he explained to his partner as he outlined his schedule to return to the office on Monday.

Unfortunately, he knew that even if he tried to disconnect, he would not entirely escape the ongoing stress of the litigation. He just hoped that he could get through the weekend without working.

That night found Sam tossing and turning once again. He lay there, his head propped up on his pillow, fingers crossed and settled on his chest. He felt his heart beating and watched his hands rise each time he breathed. He didn't want to move; didn't want to disturb Lynn, who was fast asleep next to him. It would be unfair, he thought to himself, to wreck her sleep because of his issues. So, he lay there, almost frozen in his condition, wishing for sleep but distracted by his racing thoughts.

There was a stream of nervous energy emanating from his head. He thought about his dad and the trip. He thought about his impending biopsy. He thought about work, deadlines, expectations, and the risk of failure. He thought about Lynn, Aaron, and Lucy and wanted them all to be okay. It was more than he could fit into a logical structure to settle his concerns. Instead, each issue flashed past unresolved. As the thoughts mounted, he recognized the inevitable impossibility that he would return to any sleep that night. He turned his head to see the clock on his nightstand. It was 1:30.

"Dammit," he thought. He had already acknowledged that his lack of sleep tonight would make for an impossible day tomorrow. He would be exhausted. He finally relented and slipped out of bed, trying not to wake his wife.

He used his phone's flashlight to search his wife's cabinet next to her sink. "I need an Ambien," he said to himself, though he felt like he was committing an act of burglary as he inspected each bottle. When he found the prescription bottle, he was relieved that plenty of pills were left. "Maybe she won't notice," he convinced himself. He formed a cup with his hand under the bathroom sink to add the water he needed to swallow the pill.

As he climbed back into bed, he wondered if he needed to go back to his doctor for something stronger. He did need someone to talk to. He was tired of burdening his friends and couldn't talk to Lynn. She didn't need to worry about him; she already had enough on her plate, including many of the same issues he was worrying about.

Sam breathed deeply. He exhaled by forming a circle with his lips, like he was blowing out smoke circles from a cigarette.

He would find a therapist, he said to himself. Maybe the same guy he had spoken to after his mom died. Sam was picturing their sessions, but the therapist's name had escaped his memory. He could picture the office. The chair in front of the doctor's desk. "What was his name?" Sam repeated in his head. He remembered what he looked like. The guy was middle-aged. Jewish. Bearded. Glasses. Always wore a sweater. Sam started thinking that he was remembering *Good Will Hunting* instead. He smiled. Then he breathed again. Yes. He would call that therapist. Sam needed to get back on track.

Then the Ambien kicked in.

Chapter 36

THE BUNKER HILL was on high alert. The armada was in the heavily-defended East China Sea. Max was constantly watching for planes that might release bombs on the ships or, as Japanese losses mounted, inflict kamikaze attacks. Max still did not fathom how these Japanese pilots would consent to commit suicide for the honor of their country. It was one thing to die for the fight. It was another thing to kill yourself with your plane to harm the enemy as much as possible.

Max jumped up on his bunk to get some rest after another eight-hour shift in the CIC. The carrier had moved into position with the Fifth Fleet for the final assault on Okinawa. As the ship centered its location, the crew prepared its armaments, anticipating a relentless and desperate Japanese defense. Its planes would be fueled and positioned to take off from the carrier on a moment's notice, some to support the Marine ground assault and others to defend the air attacks from Japanese fighters.

Max was tired, but it was difficult to sleep. He re-read some of Rose's letters and thought about his mother and his brother. In his bunk, he could hear the planes lift off from the deck. His bunk shook with the vibrations. Then there was the sound of the large-millimeter shells as battleships and destroyers pounded the island with their armaments.

He tried to close his eyes but could still only imagine what was happening on the island. He knew it was terrible. He just wanted it to be over. He found himself promising that if he made it through the war, he would be a good person and would make his life meaningful. He was praying. He was just hoping that God was listening.

Chapter 37

SAM WOKE UP late, at about eight o'clock. He felt refreshed. He took a shower and had some coffee with toast. He had told his dad that they would leave by nine. He was at his father's house by nine fifteen.

His dad had been waiting. "You're late," he said.

"Ten minutes. And I said, 'Around nine' anyway." Sam saw that his dad's suitcase was already waiting next to the door. "You sure you have everything?" he asked.

"Yup," his father answered.

"Meds?"

"Yup. Everything." Max seemed unconcerned.

"Glasses?"

"Yes. Enough already, let's get going."

Sam loaded up Max's suitcase into the trunk of his small BMW SUV. "I'm just going to check that the doors are all locked. I'll be back in a second," he said as he walked back towards the house. He would also make sure no appliances had been left on in the house that would cause it to burn down during their trip.

"Throw me the keys. I'll take first shift," his father yelled back.

Sam wasn't sure he heard his father clearly. Especially since Max had stopped driving ten years ago. "Dad. I'm driving," he said adamantly.

"The whole way?"

"Ha. You're kidding me, right?" Now he was a bit concerned that his father had lost his marbles.

"No. I just thought I could share the load on the driving."

"Dad, you haven't driven in a decade!" Sam reminded him.

"Not my fault. You took away my car!" Max retorted.

Sam turned to return to the house. He finished his trek through the bathrooms and the kitchen, unplugging every appliance he saw and locking the side door on his way out. That door had not been locked in a while.

Sam still wasn't sure if his dad was kidding or not about the driving, but he decided to give it a rest. "Dad. I'll take the first shift. We'll see how it goes." He watched as his father slowly made his way around to the car's passenger side. He laughed to himself as he imagined his father driving to DC. "Now, that would have been a sight," he said out loud and then hoped his father hadn't heard.

His father had a tired but sly look on his face. "Okay. But we're stopping for coffee, right?"

"Absolutely."

Sam realized that even though he had taken away his dad's keys, the state had somehow renewed his license. Sam couldn't believe it when his father told him. Sam hesitated to tell his father that he "was an accident just waiting to happen."

Sam had stayed up nights worrying about his dad's driving before he took the keys away. He had felt terrible when they had the conversation. After that, his mom ended up driving his dad to his doctor's appointments and lunches with his friends. Sam realized that it must have been tough for his dad to lose his independence like that. But it was the right call. Sam knew he didn't have a choice.

Sam got into the driver's seat and buckled his seat belt.

"All ready? All buckled up?" Sam said to his father.

His dad didn't turn to face Sam. All he said was, "I like Dunkin Donuts coffee. Black. No decaf."

Sam replied, "I know that," and backed the car out of the driveway. Maybe this was going to be a longer trip than he had expected.

His father remained quiet as they passed the mile markers along the highway. Each one seemingly came faster and faster as they continued their trip. To Sam, it felt like a metaphor for how quickly the years had also passed and led them to the place where they found themselves today.

He glanced at his father, who stared diligently out the window watching the landscape pass. Max seemed mesmerized by the flowers and trees that had budded for spring as the car sped through the Tennessee mountains. Rather than enduring the silence, Sam reached over and hit a Sirius XM button to listen to music. "How about the seventies, Dad? That was a good decade for you. Right?" He was half serious and half joking. Actually, Sam wasn't sure at all if the 1970's had been good for his father. He envisioned his dad in his fifties working to build his company. By that point, he had two young kids.

Sam recalled a picture of his dad dressed in a suit at his equipment warehouse as he gave a tour to a group of customers. Through the years, his haircut never changed; it seemed like the only thing that changed was the length of his sideburns.

His dad never wore jeans. He had said those were for the "hippies" Sam knew his dad didn't necessarily support the hippie lifestyle, and definitely not the marijuana use. But he didn't object to their statements about the war. His dad abhorred the Vietnam war. He was always pontificating for a negotiated solution to the conflict. Sam recalled him turning off the evening news each time the anchormen discussed the rising numbers of Americans lost in Vietnam or Cambodia. Sam knew that his dad had been affected by his time in World War II, so he thought he understood why he was against sending kids to war in Vietnam. Max definitely wanted his own kids to go to college to avoid getting drafted. He would tell Ben and Sam that repeatedly as they were teenagers.

A song from James Taylor ended on the "Seventies" station, and Sam could hear the guitar strokes and twanging voice of Cat Stevens as his song "Father and Son" began to play. Sam listened to the words and turned his head to see his dad. He was still focused on the view and had not responded.

"But take your time, think a lot, think of everything you've got
For you will still be here tomorrow, but your dreams
may not.
...And I know that I have to go away
I know I have to go"

Sam soaked in the song. He was shaking a bit from the impact of the words. His dad then turned his attention away from the view and focused on the radio. "Mom and I loved this music," he said. Sam noticed his dad's eyes were closed.

In that instant, Sam recognized the beauty of being with his father as he held back tears thinking about his own kids. It was unmistakable to Sam that he was coming to terms with something new that he had never really faced before. As long as his dad was here, Sam never had to face his own mortality. His dad was in the line in front of him. That was the normal process of life, but the song was about the passing of that torch from father to son and the gift of lessons passed from one generation to another. It struck Sam that maybe what scared him the most about losing his dad was that he would be next. There would be no one left in front of him. Mom, Dad, and Ben would all be gone.

As the last chord played, Sam offered to change the channel. "How about some news, Dad?"

His father didn't say a word; he only turned away again to resume watching the spring colors as they splashed across the windshield.

Sam really wanted to really talk with his dad. As they drove, there were times when Max nodded off. Other times, he just stared out the window. Sam waited for the right time to start the conversation.

After a bathroom break and some more coffee, they had just pulled back to the highway. Sam leaned over toward his father. "Dad, tell me more about Grandpa."

Max hesitated for a moment, gathering his thoughts, gathering his memories. "He died when I was twelve," he said.

"Baruch was his name?" Sam asked, already knowing the answer.

"Yes," his father replied. "Ben was named after him. He was a religious man. He had been preparing me for my bar mitzvah when he passed."

"Remind me what your father did for work?"

"He worked on the docks. Not glamorous, but plenty of work. He had worked his way up to being a foreman. He was a strong, strong man. I remember him flexing his muscles to show off for my mother. When he wasn't working or sleeping, he would hang out on the street with my brother and me, playing catch. He was a good man. It was not an easy thing growing up on the Lower East Side. You had to be strong, not just in strength but in character. I wanted to be as strong a man as he was."

"And your mom?" Sam asked.

"She was just pure love," his father said, a smile returning to his face. "She had come to the country as an immigrant. With nothing. She met my father..." He stumbled with his words, then said, "Actually, she was matched with my father when she was just 18. But she was the best. She took care of him. Cooked, cleaned for him, adored him. She was heartbroken when he died. All of us were. But she managed to survive. My uncle was successful. He had started a clothing business and opened a number of stores. He paid for her and for us to live. She never remarried. Probably should have, but never did."

Then he went on.

"When I got married, she was so happy. She loved your mom. They sometimes acted more like sisters than how a mother-in-law acted in those days. Rose had a difficult relationship with her own parents."

"And your uncle?"

"Shimon. Another amazing man," Max said. "My uncle helped me to finish studying for my bar mitzvah after my father died. He stood beside me when I first read from the Torah. He started as a peddler, as many of them did. But he was so smart. He started a distribution business with men from other boroughs. They would trade and share profits."

"Did he ever make the clothing or just sell it?' Sam inquired.

"Eventually, he leased a building and started making men's suits. I was just a kid. But I got a new suit for my bar mitzvah."

Sam laughed. "That must have been quite a sight."

"Your great-uncle Shimon was the reason I survived high school. We were a close-knit family back then. Everyone took care of each other. We were lucky. But after high school, I enlisted, and when I got back, everything changed. I married your mom, moved to Nashville…you know the rest."

Sam nodded. "I do," before pausing and adding, "I know you named me after him. After Great Uncle Shimon."

"Yes," his dad replied. "May his memory be a blessing."

Sam looked at his dad. Now, more than ever, it seemed that both he and his father were "on the clock." Father and son together again. Hopefully, this would be a time to tie up loose ends. There weren't many. Over the years, both had verbally expressed how they felt about each other. They were in a good place. There were things that would never change, no matter how much they talked about them. Now, it was a time for them to simply be together.

Chapter 38

WORD STARTED COMING through the crew that the war in Europe was almost over. The Russians had advanced against Germany on the eastern front, and the British, French, and Americans were approaching Berlin. Stories were now spreading quickly about the liberation of Paris and the rescue of Jews from the German concentration camps. Hitler was being defeated. It seemed like only good news was coming from the Atlantic and Europe.

Again, Max thought about Jacob. Europe seemed a distant planet from where Max was right now. Max wondered where his older brother was and how he was. He was certain that he was still alive. Max saw Jacob as strong and confident. He thought back to the days when they were both younger and carefree—no war in their lives.

Max pictured Jacob on the front stoop of their apartment building in New York. He was pulling a baseball from his jacket pocket and sailing the ball into the waiting glove of his brother. The two boys, only two years apart, maintained this ritual of playing catch after dinner in the street in front of their apartment building almost every night, sometimes in the rain, sometimes even in the snow. Jacob was older, but Max was big for his age. There were many times the neighbors could not tell the boys apart.

"Wear your coats!" their mother would shout as they ran from the apartment and down the four flights to the street below.

Tossing the ball back and forth was a ritual between them. The brothers would each talk, distracted by the physical focus of watching the ball reach their glove, removing it with their free hand, and measuring the distance between them to calculate the proper arc and strength of the next throw.

When they were younger, the discussions were often not more than the ongoing exploits of comic book characters they read about or the recent achievements of their heroes on the baseball field, each of them diehard Brooklyn Dodgers fans. As they got older, they talked about life and what they wanted to do after high school. But then the war came.

Max remembered his mother at the train station when Jacob left for basic training. Jacob hugged and kissed her before boarding the train. Max remembered how his mother had cried. She had lost her husband already. Now she was sending her oldest son off to war. The last words he heard his mother say to Jacob that day was, "Keep your head down!" Max hoped his brother had listened.

Chapter 39

AS THEY WERE driving, Sam couldn't help but think of Ben. Ben would have loved this road trip with his dad.

It wasn't all bad with Ben. They were brothers. The five-year difference made it a bit strange when they were younger. Back then, Sam idolized his older brother. He would follow him everywhere. Sam would seek to emulate Ben's mannerisms, dress, likes, and dislikes, including sports teams and music.

It was probably the worst when Ben was in high school and Sam was still in elementary school. Sam followed Ben everywhere, even when Ben was discovering girls. Sam would sneak up on Ben when he was making out with some girl in the yard behind their house. Once, he even barged into Ben's room while their parents were out, and Ben was supposed to be babysitting. Sam laughed as he remembered his brother hog-tying him with a belt to keep Sam in his room while Ben went back to "necking" in his room. Ben didn't seem to care when Sam threatened to "Tell Mom and Dad" when they got home. Ben tended to push back against his parents and test their limits. It got worse as he got older. He was not a good student and started hanging out with the wrong crowd. It was a spiral that Sam's parents could not stop. They were not prepared to handle a kid like Ben.

Ben met Trish when they were both still in high school. Both had been loners that seemed to find each other. Now, they spent all their time together, listening to records and playing their guitars together. They were in love. His parents talked with Trish's parents about how much time they were spending with each other, the missed classes in school, and the drugs they found in their kid's bedrooms.

Ben and Trish argued with their parents about their age, their independence, and their plan for adventures in life. It was 1968. They took the car that Ben had bought from cutting lawns and doing odd jobs and drove west without graduating. They wanted to be in California. Ben had taken his draft card with him. His parents weren't even certain that if his number was called that he would enlist.

The night they left, Sam remembered his mother crying. It was not the last time she would cry over Ben. His parents had reported their leaving to the police, but they couldn't do anything about it since they were both eighteen. Max had not been much older when he had left for the war. But this would be a different type of war. The enemy was the culture. It couldn't be stopped unless Ben wanted to stop.

Sam knew that he would not follow his brother's footsteps this time. He couldn't bear to see his mother like this. He would take a different path.

When Sam got to high school, Ben had been on the road with Trish for a few years, but Sam and Ben saw each other occasionally. Whenever Ben was back in town, he would take his little brother to his friend's houses to party. Ben would get Sam a beer to drink or even offer him a drag from a weed cigarette. There were no limitations in Ben's world at the time. He was invincible.

Those were tough years for Max and Rose. They felt like failures. They wanted Ben to be happy. But the risks were too great.

Sam loved his older brother. Sometimes he admired him for his zest for life and his hypnotic energy. There was the laugh, the exuberant joy that came from the smallest things. He would make Sam laugh all the time. While everything was serious to Sam, nothing was serious to Ben. But there was the excess too. He was never without a drink or a smoke. There was always the reality of drugs, whether pot or another stimulant. It was how he coped.

There was a time Ben visited Sam when Sam was in college. Ben was the guy who bought the bottle of vodka to the party. He was the life of the party until he wasn't. Ben got so drunk and boisterous that Sam left early, embarrassed to be seen with his older brother.

During those years, Sam saw the pain in his mother's eyes. The constant worry. The fear of the unknown. There were also times when Ben was larger than life and made his mom and dad smile. He always had grand plans and successful projects. He was everyone's best friend. You felt loved by him.

Essentially, there was no middle for Ben. It was either up or down. Ben had once told Sam that he thought he would "live fast and die young" like James Dean. That always bothered Sam because he couldn't understand why his brother would want to squander away his life.

It was things like that which emphasized the disconnect between them. Sam and Ben were clearly different people. Maybe it was the age or the attitude, but Sam didn't want the noise, the clutter, the dissonance. He longed for the quiet and the simplicity of life.

And as they got older, the more-responsible Sam distanced himself from the more-irresponsible Ben. His parents played the middle, always hoping to keep the family together. But Sam also recalled the times when his dad reached his limit. Once, he threatened to throw Ben out of the house, to disown him as a son. Those were terrible times for his parents.

Sam tried to imagine a point that far into a parent's despair, with no choice but to separate yourself from your own child. And his mother. His poor mother. Silent in the battle. Crying and alone. A desperate witness to the unfolding accident but powerless to intercede. There were a lot of tears over the years as Ben created untold fears for them of what could happen to their son. Sometimes, even as a kid, Sam understood the sadness that overcame his parents as Ben disappeared for days at a time. They didn't know whether he was dead or alive. He knew his mother tortured herself with those memories up until the day she died.

Ben and Trish were together for almost ten years before she left him. He begged her to stay, but she realized that all he could do was offer promises that would never be fulfilled. She loved him, but he would not be enough, so she packed a bag and left.

Ben had no way to survive without her. He was lost. He came back to Nashville. He had no high school degree and no job. His parents let him move back into the house for a while before he left to live with friends. His father would often say that "Ben was lost." And that "He'll need to find himself before we can help him."

Chapter 40

VICTORY WAS PROCLAIMED in Europe on May 8, 1945. The word spread quickly through the crew of the Bunker Hill. Hitler was dead, and they were celebrating around the world.

Max wondered about Jacob. There had been no news. Max hope that "no news is good news" as it related to his brother. Again, Max envisioned Jacob drinking champagne somewhere near the Arc de Triomphe strolling along the Champs-Élysées with his army buddies. He missed Jacob and longed for a time where they could be together again back home.

Max relented that the war in the Pacific would have to continue until the Japanese surrendered or were destroyed. The Marines continued to advance toward the historic Shuri Castle on the Island of Okinawa, where the Japanese had now anchored their defenses. Tens of thousands of Okinawan civilians were forced to join the battle against the Americans, and casualties were mounting on both sides.

His celebration about the news lasted only minutes when again the general alarm returned and orders to return to "battle stations" blared over the speakers. Max ran to the CIC. Another attack. More bombs. More death.

Chapter 41

I T WAS A slow leak. Sam knew by the way that the steering wheel was pulling that the tire was losing air. They had just passed Roanoke. It was just a matter of whether he could make it to Charlottesville, where Sam had made their hotel reservation for the night. That would only leave a few hours for them to drive to DC on Saturday morning.

He told his dad that he thought they had a flat. He didn't want to worry him, but he knew it would. Then he took the next exit, near a town called White Pine, and pulled off the road to check the damage to the right front tire. As Sam made his way around the front of the car, his father opened the passenger door and made a strong effort to exit.

"Dad. Just stay in the car. I'm just checking the tire."

"I have to piss," his dad said.

Sam looked around. "Well, I guess this place is as good as any."

He was right: The tire was down but not out. He didn't see a nail but figured he had driven over something to cause a puncture. He then heard the stream of water coming from behind him.

"Watch out for snakes," Sam joked with his father.

"Very funny," his dad answered. "Watch out, one day you won't be able to go anywhere without a diaper either!"

Sam smiled.

"You need help to get back?" Sam watched his father zip up and slowly move toward the car. He had traveled less than five feet.

"No. Should be okay."

"No walker?" Sam asked.

"No time. Nature called." His father took two more steps, looked at the tire, and then at his son. "You going to change it?" he asked.

"No, are you?" his son quickly answered.

"Very funny. Do you even know how to change a flat?'

"Yes. Call AAA," Sam said with a sneer.

"I have obviously failed you as a father." Max sat back down in the car.

"We need to drive into town and get it fixed," Sam said. "We'll patch it, and then I'll deal with a new tire when we get home."

"Suits me," said Max. "So long as we get there in one piece."

Sam laughed. "No guarantees."

Sam got back into the car and took the next exit. He drove slowly and cautiously until he found a gas station near the exit. Sam went into the station to talk to the attendant. They had an open bay and had agreed to check the tire. Sam offered to pay for a new tire if it was needed.

While Max sat in the lobby of the garage, Sam walked outside to call his office. He didn't want to but knew that he had to. The case was moving along, and all he wanted was for his team to keep it afloat until he got back to town on Monday. "Push as much as you can into next week," Sam ordered. "File any extensions that you need."

"Everything okay, Sam?" his father asked as he walked back inside.

"Yup. just the normal craziness. They say anything about the car?"

"They said you should have bought American," his father replied.

"You're like Henny Youngman today!"

"And here I thought you were the one full of one-liners," his dad replied, adding, "I don't remember getting any flats on the Cadillac."

Sam laughed. His dad always bought American cars. Never German or Japanese. Not after the war. Sam assumed he never forgave them. He was a one-man boycott. He wasn't happy when Sam bought his BMW.

But Sam thought about the Caddy that his dad drove for years until Sam took away the keys. His dad never got a flat because he never drove more than ten miles a day. Sam remained amazed that his father never got into an accident. He was a lousy driver.

"I loved that Caddy," he said to his father.

They sat in the waiting room for a little while. Max was starting to doze off. He would snore when he slept. Sam was uncomfortable with his father falling asleep in the gas station lobby.

"So, Dad," he said. "What was Nashville like when you moved there?

His father took a minute to clear his cobwebs from his short nap. "Such a small town back then," he started. "We were pioneers."

"What about the Jewish community?" his son asked, part of the ongoing history lesson Sam was getting as part of their drive together.

"Well, it's not like we were the first Jews to move into town. There were already a few small synagogues and even the start of a Jewish Community Center. We moved here in 1950, just after Ben was born."

"Were you always members of Temple Shalom?" Sam remembered his years of Hebrew School when he was younger and his bar mitzvah at thirteen.

"Yes. Since we first moved to town. We joined shortly after it moved from its original location to west Nashville. Did you know it was founded in 1876?"

Sam nodded. Sam remembered his younger years at the synagogue growing up.

Max began to tell a story about the synagogue. Although Sam knew the story, his father told it to him as if he was telling it for the first time.

"In 1958, a bomb went off at the Jewish Community Center, and then there were threats made at our temple because our rabbi had been vocal about civil rights and integration. With a name like 'Silver,' it wasn't that my customers didn't know I was Jewish. I had my share of bigoted and racist customers. But as long as we did our job, everyone got along."

Sam knew that his lack of commitment to a Jewish life had

disappointed his parents. Again, with everything that was happening, Sam wondered if it was too late for him to try again. He felt like he was missing something in his life. Maybe it was the spirituality that came with believing in God, any god.

"Those were challenging times in the community," his father said. "The Jews were still a small minority. But the numbers really changed over the years." His father's voice trembled a bit. "I'm happy we moved here. The city has grown a lot in the last fifty years, the Jewish community as well." His father spoke with pride. Although they had not been the first, they were part of the group that had helped the community grow. Both he and Rose had been active members of both their synagogue and other organizations.

"I read recently that Nashville is the largest Jewish community in Tennessee," Sam said. "Surprising that it's even larger than Memphis."

"Lots of newer synagogues, both in the city and the suburbs," said Max.

"And did I tell you that Dinah Shore grew up here?" his dad added.

"Yes, Dad. I know all about it."

"The most famous Jew from Nashville!" his father would say.

Sam laughed. Max loved to remind people about her. Sam assumed that he knew her personally, but his dad was never clear about that.

Sam wasn't sure how much things had really changed in the last fifty years. Whether in Nashville or New York, there were divisions. Jewish, non-Jewish, white, Black, Democratic, and Republican walls were being put up figuratively all the time. He thought about how little he had done to help bridge the divide. There was so much more that needed to be done. Sam admonished himself that he had sat on the sidelines, focusing only on his career. He knew it was selfish.

The flat tire had only delayed them an hour before they were back on the road and on their way to Charlottesville. They checked into the hotel a little after six that night, and Sam's phone rang as he put their hotel key into the door.

It was the office.

Sam hesitated but took the call as he fumbled with his suitcase into the room. "Hey, Jack. What's up?" He knew that it would probably not be good news from his partner.

"Sam, problem with one of our witnesses."

"What now?" Sam asked as he escorted his father into the hotel room and dropped his suitcase on one of the two queen beds.

"Seems to be recanting his testimony."

"We can depose him if we have to," Sam answered, trying to find a quick solution and move on.

"The client's looking for you. They want you here to walk them through the options."

Sam hesitated. He knew what he would have done before and what he had done many times in the past. He would give up his personal time, his family time, and go back to work. He was the problem-solver. That's what he did.

But this time was different. He couldn't. He knew that. They would have to wait. They would have to understand, he explained to his partner.

"Understand what?" said Jack. "There is no 'understanding' from these guys. Bad result, and you get a malpractice claim."

"I can't believe I'm hearing this," Sam said. "Look. We just got here. I can't work on this. Not now. I'll be back Monday. It will have to wait."

"I'll do what I can," Jack said, adding, "but it's on you." Then he hung up.

"Dammit!" They were asking him to choose between work and his family again. He was angry at them and then at himself—because, for a moment, he found himself thinking about the choice. How did he ever become a person who would even consider leaving his dad in the middle of a trip to go back to work?

"What's wrong, Sam?" asked his father.

"It's fine. Really, Dad. It's just work. It's always something happening over there."

"You are allowed a few days off, son," his father said.

"I know that Dad. It just gets to me when I think I'm letting people down."

His father sat quietly for a minute, considering his response. The comment hung in the air for what seemed like forever as he gathered his thoughts.

"When you hit ninety," his father said, "it gives you a little perspective on priorities."

"I understand, Dad."

"No. Let me finish." A bit of sternness in his voice.

"The only people you can ever let down are the people you love and who love you. Those are the only people who really matter in this world. The rest are just pieces of life's story. Unfortunately, no matter what we think, we are interchangeable pieces that can be fixed or replaced. So, it's Lynn, Aaron, and Lucy that you need to worry about."

"How about you, Dad?"

"You can never disappoint me, son. Not possible."

Sam looked at his dad and understood the sense of unconditional love that a parent has for their children. "No matter how hard I try?" he asked with a smile.

"Ha!" his father exclaimed. "I thought you were trying all these years."

Sam laughed. "Got it, Dad. Got it." His dad's words carried him to thoughts of Aaron and Lucy. Then he changed the subject. "Enough about work. How about food? You hungry?"

"Sure," his dad replied.

Sam and Max walked to the elevator and returned to the lobby. Sam made his way over to the front desk concierge. "We need a place to eat nearby. Something local. Nice, but not too nice. Better than a Sizzler."

The concierge looked up from his desk. Clearly, he had no idea what a "Sizzler" was, but he got Sam's drift regardless.

The man called and made their reservations. Sam went to get the car from the self-park and picked his father out in front of the hotel.

After they got to the restaurant Max used his walker to get through the restaurant. They were seated in a booth near the windows.

"Thanks," Sam nodded to the hostess as she moved the walker to a nearby alcove.

"Have a nice dinner," she replied.

Sam opened the menu and agreed with the concierge that the options were extensive. "I don't know about you, Dad, but I'm hungry," Sam said.

Sam then opened the cocktail menu and added, "And thirsty."

Max opened his menu as well. When the waiter came by, Sam ordered a bourbon, neat, and asked his dad if he wanted to join him.

"Not tonight, thank you," his father said, covered by the large menu.

"Can we order, too?' Sam asked the waiter. "Dad, you ready?"

"Just give me a minute."

After the waiter left, the two of them sat in the booth. Sam checked his phone for further e-mails and was relieved when his drink arrived.

"Cheers, Dad," Sam said as he raised his glass and took his first gulp. Sam didn't realize how much he'd needed that drink. "Long day, Dad. How're you doing?" He asked partly out of concern and partly to break the silence.

"Just thinking," his father replied, "but it was a nice day."

"I'm glad you wanted to do this," Sam said. "Nice to get away for a few days. I could certainly use the break."

More silence.

"So, what's your thought on the rest of the season?" Sam asked, trying a new topic.

Max was slow to respond. "Baseball?"

"Yes," Sam said. "Have you not been watching?"

"Not much."

Sam was surprised. "Dad, you love baseball. I thought you had been watching some games?"

"On too late for me."

Sam hesitated. They had loved watching the Braves over the last few years. They had even made a trip to Atlanta about ten years before, right after Sam had moved back. His dad had grown up as a Dodgers fan but had settled on the Braves as the nearest option when they moved to Atlanta in the sixties.

But his dad was right. The games were on late, and Sam had made no effort since the season had started even to watch one with his dad. He felt a twinge of sadness, realizing that he had missed that time together.

"Greatest player?" Sam asked, trying to spark up the conversation.

Max was quiet. Sam wasn't sure if he'd take the bait. He knew his dad was nervous about the reunion.

"Hank Aaron," his dad said. "And Joe DiMaggio. You'll never see the likes of those players again."

"No? What about guys like Griffey? McGwire?"

"Different time. The games are different. Power over finesse."

"True. All about the home run," Sam said, with deference to his dad.

There was quiet.

"Greatest game?" Sam asked.

"What?" his dad turned to his son.

"Greatest game ever played?"

"Well, you know the answer to that." Max replied.

"The shot heard 'round the world". Bobby Thompson. World Series."

"Hey, that was a home run, too," he reminded his father.

"Smart aleck!" his dad said and smiled.

Sam smiled back.

He knew he could always talk baseball with his dad. It was one of those bonds they had. Something they both loved. Something they used to share. When he was younger, his dad would toss the ball with him in his backyard. He taught him how to soften his glove with oil and worked with him and Ben on throwing to a target. It was baseball. It had its own language and its own energy. It was fun. It was a game.

Sam turned his eyes toward his dad. Max Silver was not the man he used to be. Age had taken his stature and his strength. There would be no more balls tossed in the yard. No more visits to the ballpark. It was too hard, too challenging. Time had passed.

"Dad, we have not really ever talked about this, but for all these years you've experienced and everything you've seen, don't you feel like you have lessons to teach? Values that you want to share? At least for Aaron and Lucy? They would love to know some of your stories."

His father sat quietly. Sam wasn't sure if he had heard him or maybe didn't understand what he was asking. He was talking about an ethical will—a story, a lesson learned, an experience that needed to be passed on. Sam understood the concept because there were things he wished that he had talked about with his mom. But now it was too late. Here was an opportunity to talk about these things with his father, who had ninety years of stories and lessons. Sam would be making a mistake not to ask for them.

Just then, the food arrived. It probably was just in time. His dad looked tired. It had been a long day. Max needed his rest before the reunion tomorrow.

When they returned to the hotel room, it was only 9:00. It was still early. Max said he was going to wash up and go to bed. Sam said he was going down to the lobby to make some calls.

As he reached the ground floor, Sam pressed the number for his wife.

"Sam? Everything okay?" Lynn asked before she even said hello.

"Yes. Fine. We just went straight to dinner. Ended up at some steak place. It was fine. He hardly ate."

"And you?" his wife asked. "How was the drive? You must be exhausted."

"I'm fine. Dad slept a lot of the way. But we did talk."

"Anything new?" his wife asked.

"Nope. He does seem a bit pensive about the reunion, but otherwise good."

"Will you call me after?"

"Yes. I'll call you tomorrow. Good night."

"Good night," she answered. "Love you." She ended every conversation that way. He found it empowering that she was willing to express herself and show her love demonstrably. Sam tried, but it was different for him. He dialed his son's number.

After a few rings, the voicemail began. "Hi, It's Aaron. Leave me a message or text me."

Sam hit "End Call." He was not going to leave another message.

When he returned to the room, his father was already asleep. After he washed up, Sam climbed into the adjacent bed and checked his phone one last time before trying to sleep. It was eleven o'clock. They had agreed to pack up and drive by nine the following day. It would take them a couple of hours to get to DC for the event, which was scheduled to start at one. Even if they hit traffic, they would get there in time.

Chapter 42

ON MAY 11, 1945, the Bunker Hill was operating within Task Force Fifty-Eight between Okinawa and the sacred soil of the southernmost tip of Kyushu in the Japanese homeland. Kamikaze attacks were now a common part of everyday life. Even as the crew witnessed some of their sister ships being hit, they had come to expect the suicide attacks, just as they expected to get up each morning at dawn to send the Corsairs on their strikes against the Japanese forces on Okinawa.

At nine that morning, Max arrived to relieve the overnight crew and take his place on the radar watch. The CIC was the ship's eyes and ears. If there were enemy planes in the area, it was Max's job to announce the vector and alert the carrier crew, which would then pass the information to its pilots and the other ships in the area. He always feared he would miss something, and he remained vigilant for anything he saw on his screen.

This would be a day that Max would never forget. It would ultimately define who he was for the rest of his life.

Chapter 43

IT WAS 2:00 in the morning. Sam woke, startled to the sounds of his father's loud muttering. He sounded as if he were trying to scream. Sam sat up in bed and watched for a moment as his father fought the monsters in his dreams. Then Sam got up and starting shaking his father's shoulder. "Dad, Dad, wake up," he said softly but clearly.

"What? What?" was his father's startled reaction.

"Dad, you were having a bad dream," Sam said.

At that moment, his father recognized where he had been in his dream. He had been back on the ship, with the same fear and astonishment that flowed through his bones over seventy years ago. He had returned, once again, to that moment in time that he could not escape, no matter how he tried.

"Dad, what is it? What was the dream?" his son asked out of concern and curiosity.

"Nothing. Nothing," his father replied. "Go back to bed!" His father seemed angry or maybe even afraid. He then rolled over and returned to a fetal position with his back to Sam.

Sam waited quietly as his father dozed off again. Sam stood and walked to the other side of the room to watch his father and ensure he was okay.

Sam couldn't help but study his father's face as he slept. Sam wondered about the dream. What had he seen or experienced that gave him such fear? But Sam wasn't sure he could ever ask his father that question. It would be a part of him that he likely would never know.

Sam wanted to call Lynn about his father's behavior. But he chose not to let her know. He shared everything with his wife. But sometimes, he felt like she had heard enough and that he didn't need to burden her with one more aspect of Sam's anxiety, his worries, his fears. He knew that he would hold back telling her the details of this trip, except for the pictures of him and his dad, the "selfies" of their road trip.

Sam patterned his marriage after what he witnessed with his father and his mother. They had been married for more than 65 years when his mom passed. He never heard a cross word between them. He wanted to emulate their relationship.

Eventually, he fell back asleep. He woke up the next morning at seven from his cell phone buzzing—messages from work. On top of everything else, the case was ramping up, and Sam felt bombarded with questions about the lawsuit that he felt pressured to answer. He put on some sweats and running shoes and tried to leave the room quietly to send his responses and make some calls.

"Sam?" his father said, unsure whether Sam was still in the room.

"Yup. I was just heading to the lobby. Maybe some coffee and toast before we hit the road?"

"Yes. Sounds good. I need some coffee," his father answered. "Black."

"Yeah. Got it." Sam quietly closed the door behind him. He called his wife as he walked out of the elevator into the lobby.

"Hi, honey," Sam said as Lynn answered.

"Hi," she said. "How are you? How's your dad?"

"Fine," Sam replied. "I think he's nervous about today. I think he had some bad dreams last night."

"Wow, did he talk about them?"

"Have you met my dad?" Sam said sarcastically. He knew his father wouldn't talk about it. "It will be interesting to see how he handles all of this today."

"What about you?"

"I'm just pissed about the office. Apparently, the case preparation is going south, and the client wants me to help right the ship. I told them no."

"Good for you," she said.

"Remind me you said that after we have to sell the house and live in our car!" Sam again sarcastically responded. He always worried about the risk of failure.

"When do you leave for DC?" she asked, ignoring her husband's comment.

"I'm just in the lobby to get some coffee and to answer some e-mails. We have to get out of here by 9:30 at the latest. I'm hoping there is not a lot of traffic to deal with."

"Call me later to let me know how it went," she asked.

He was equally curious as to how the day would unfold. "Will do. Bye," he said, adding, "Love you," in anticipation of her response.

Sam ordered the coffees and sat down at a nearby table to send some e-mails as he waited. In a few moments, he heard his name, retrieved the two coffees, and headed back to the room. When he walked in, his father was already dressed.

"Looking good, Dad!" Sam said. His father was in a suit and tie. But Sam could also see the sadness in his father's eyes.

"I wish your mom were here to see this," his dad said.

Sam heard the emptiness in his voice.

"Sorry, Dad. But she's with you for this. We both are."

Sam helped his father load the walker into the back seat, and his father climbed into the car's passenger seat. They would need about two hours to get the DC to arrive in time for the ceremony.

"You okay, Dad?" His son asked as he turned the key to start the car.

"Fine. Let's just get there." Max replied. Sam knew not to offer any follow-up comments. His father was either nervous or upset. Sam thought better than to add to the moment's stress.

It was quiet most of the way to DC, other than the songs playing on the car radio.

Again, Sam found himself thinking about Ben. It was hard for Sam to turn off his memories of Ben. Some were still so clear to him that they felt like they had happened yesterday. Images of Ben fluttered in his head.

He remembered one time when Ben called him about an investment. When Ben called, it wasn't just to "check in," ask about the kids or invite Sam to a ball game. His calls were about money, a problem, or even, as had happened before, an arrest. Sam had to be in the right frame of mind to take the call. He remembered one conversation in particular. His brother had called him at work. Sam was rushed but was alarmed that his brother was calling. He answered the phone.

"Hey, Ben. I've got a minute between meetings," Sam said as he took the call during work, cautioning his brother from the outset that his time was short. "Everything alright?"

"All is good," his older brother answered. "All good," he repeated.

"So, what's up?" Sam asked impatiently.

"I need you to talk to Dad for me."

"About what?"

"Great investment opportunity. Friend of mine. Terrific stock tip. Trying to get Dad to invest. Put in a piece for me as the go-between. Stock is supposed to fly. Can't lose." Ben always seemed to be desperately looking for a "get rich quick" scheme. He thought things came easy.

"Dad's not going to do that," Sam said. "He's coupon-cutting these days."

"Damn! He's sitting on a bundle. House alone is worth half a million. He doesn't need it. It's my inheritance anyway. Just want him to shake a little of it loose now," his brother said almost matter-of-factly, like it was a proper estate management practice.

"Or you could get a job," Sam responded, "and you could leave Mom and Dad alone."

"I have a job," his brother responded. "I don't have *your* job, but I make plenty. I'm managing the bar now. Pulling tips like crazy on weekends." He paused. "But maybe you can get me something at your firm. Something during the day?"

"As a lawyer?" Sam responded like it was a joke. But he knew that he had done it again. Sam had insulted his older brother.

"Screw you, little brother. Just talk to Dad. But don't say anything to Mom. She's got enough going on."

Sam knew that Ben was worried about Mom too. If nothing, he lived with his heart on his sleeve. He really did have a soft side. "How much do you need?" he asked.

"Ten thousand would be great."

"Are you fucking kidding me?" he blurted before realizing that he had sworn out loud and some of his staff had heard him. Then he hesitated. He knew what he would have to do. "I'll put something together for you. We'll call it a loan. You can pay me back after you sell the stock." As Sam said the words, he knew it was only to buy some peace. He didn't know if the money was for the stock, rent, or drugs. He had stopped caring. He had given up.

That had been only a few weeks before Mom had died. Thinking back, Sam assumed it had been for drugs. *Brothers*, he thought to himself. No family is perfect. Some just hide it better.

Thinking about Ben was stressful for Sam in so many ways. But it was also life. Sam understood that everyone had their challenges in life. It was just another battle to try to make your life the best that you can. And that was what Sam was doing now: He was fighting his dad's last battle beside him. Sam felt right about it.

Chapter 44

THE FIRST REPORT of an enemy plane in the area came in at about 9:30 and was promptly dealt with. The planes from the ship that were already airborne were quickly dispatched. Max knew the US planes would focus their attack on the enemy "bogey" identified from the radar. Max could track the American Corsair jet on his radar as it turned to bear down on the slower Japanese fighter. As he watched his screen, he heard the report over the CIC intercom confirm that the "meatball" had been "splashed." The positive news heightened the energy in the CIC. After some congratulatory cheers, the focus returned to the radar scanners and plotting of the departing planes.

With the tenseness relaxed, the energy level became normal again. Max understood that this did not mean anyone was dropping their guard; they were just using the time to recover. Max thought that the comparison to a professional fighter would be the best description of the men in the CIC. He understood that although they were tuned and primed for their fight, they would also take advantage of every moment of rest they could find between rounds.

Chapter 45

T HEY WERE LESS than thirty minutes outside of DC. Sam looked over at his dad. As he thought about the upcoming reunion, he thought it would be impossible for him to understand his father. There was too much that Max would never share. The dangers of war, losing friends, maintaining his business, providing for his family, the loss of his mom, and Ben's death. Sam wasn't sure why he tried so hard to get into his dad's head about these things. They were all about his dad's life, not his. It wasn't for him to know. But he so wanted to understand his father, as if the clarity of the man's experiences would somehow protect Sam from challenges that would likely lie ahead for him.

Sam had hoped to find a greater connection with his dad by sharing the trip. Maybe he looked forward to this time because he was starting to forget his mother. It had only been five years, but it seemed longer. It was as if he felt less of her presence with every day that went by. Her face was often blurred for him. How could he forget her?

Sam thought about his kids. What would they remember about him once he was gone?

Sam broke the silence. "I could use some advice on dealing with the kids," he said.

It took a minute, but his father finally responded. "There's no playbook on parenting." Max looked over at his son. "All you can do is provide your support and guidance. At some point, they go and live their own lives."

"Like I did…when I left?" Sam asked.

"Your mother and I were happy for you. Proud of you."

"But I left," Sam said as an admission.

"Yes, you did. But then you came back. The last ten years were a blessing for us. And I think you have forgiven yourself a bit, haven't you?"

"Maybe," Sam said. "I'm worried about Aaron. I want him to be free and independent, but I feel like I've lost him. I guess I feel guilty about that."

"Your mother was an expert on guilt. You certainly have her genes," said Max, "Listen, you need to let it run its course. It's not that he doesn't love you and Lynn. It's just that he has to figure out his own way. Again, just like you did."

His father was careful not to preach to his son.

"But I wasn't here until after Mom got sick and after it was too late for Ben."

"That's God's plan. You need to move on. Let it be," his father said softly.

"I guess I am overreacting about Aaron. But I think I've pushed him too much or expect too much from him."

"Maybe you do. But that's okay. We are all the product of our parents, good or bad," his dad explained. Then he looked at his son and said, "Just love your kids, and everything will fall into place."

Those words were meaningful for Sam. A bit of the wisdom that he was looking for from his father. It was becoming clear to Sam that, at the end of the day, it was all about family. Although he still had a way to go, he knew in his heart that life was all whom you love and who loves you—nothing more, nothing less.

Sam and Lynn had done everything they could to make a life for their kids. They wanted each of them to get the best education possible and find careers they would enjoy and thrive in. They had hoped the move to Nashville would not only be good for Sam and Lynn as children for their parents but as parents for their children. But Nashville was not for Aaron like it was for Lucy. Maybe it was because Lucy had gotten the chance to go to High School there while Aaron had left almost right away for college.

Aaron was always moving forward and not looking back. Although Sam and Lynn were worried about him, they never stopped believing in him. They felt like he would be okay even if the road along the way may have been difficult. But it disappointed them that his visits home were limited to Christmas-time and maybe a trip home during the summer. Lucy had stayed more connected. Aaron had created a life separate from his family. Sam missed his son.

Soon Sam saw some of the Washington memorials as they got closer to the Mall. The Jefferson Memorial was on their right, and the Lincoln Memorial was on their left. Sam turned to his father and said, "Interesting to be in DC right now." Then Sam offered, "Want to swing by and say hello to the president?"

His father didn't flinch. "Lincoln was a great president. Equal to FDR and Ike. I haven't been a fan of any of them since Ike."

Sam laughed, "That's a while ago, dad. Did you vote for any of them?"

"Sure, I did. But it seemed like most of the time, we were picking the best of the worst. Wasn't always like that." Then Max added, "As you know, I'm not a fan of politics."

"Yes. I was aware of that," Sam said with a smile. Then he added, "So what do you remember about Ike?"

"He was a leader, not a politician. We needed some guidance as a country after the war. We needed leadership. He was a true leader. We felt safe with him."

His father looked at him. "He understood war. Dealing with the enemy. It all could have been a lot worse."

"Like Vietnam?" Sam asked.

"A waste of lives," his dad said. "To fight what? A red wave. That was Johnson's fault; he should never have been president."

It struck Sam, maybe for the first time, that his dad was the only person he knew that had been alive through so many presidents. So many decades. It was an amazing walk through history. It had not been a topic that Sam thought of often, but his dad was alive to watch the evolution of cars, planes, computers, and the internet. Almost a century of change, of challenge, of recovery.

He had lived through so much. What an amazing life, Sam thought to himself.

Sam followed the map system in his car until he saw a sign for the event with directions for disabled parking. They had made it with time to spare. Sam felt relieved.

As he looked around for the entrance, Sam realized that anyone attending the reunion would likely use the disability parking areas or at least the parking location as a drop-off point. Since they had gotten there early, one of the military escorts directed them to a spot where he could park the car so that his dad would not have far to walk.

As his dad exited the car, the military attendant offered him the option of a wheelchair, which he refused.

"Dad, you sure? That's a lot of walking." Sam was being passive-aggressive. He wanted his dad to use the wheelchair to make it easier for himself. He hated the "slow walk."

"I'm fine." His dad was quick and short in his response. There would be no room for arguing with him about anything today.

Sam was excited that the ceremony would take place at the World War II Memorial. He had never been. It had opened in 2004. Sam realized that he had not been back to DC in over a decade.

Sam escorted his dad up the accessible ramp to the middle of the semi-circular structure. Sam saw tents erected in one of the corners with patriotic bunting and a banner that read "In Honor of the Men and Families of the USS Bunker Hill." Sam glanced around the large Memorial. He had previously skimmed through a Google search and other sites to learn what he could about the Memorial before their trip, but now he struggled with his recall. As he viewed the area, he remembered that over seven acres had been dedicated to the Memorial, which honored the nation's battles against Germany in the Atlantic and Japan in the Pacific.

As his eyes traveled from one granite pillar to another, he remembered that there were 56 in total, each inscribed with the name of the 48 states in 1945, plus the District of Columbia, the

Alaska Territory, the Territory of Hawaii, the Commonwealth of the Philippines, Puerto Rico, Guam, American Samoa, and the US Virgin Islands. There were two arches, one titled the "Atlantic" and the other the "Pacific," and relief scenes from both the European and Pacific theaters.

Sam slowly walked with his father along the ramp of the Pacific path, passing the themed art sculptures that framed the walkway, beginning with a piece titled "Enlistment," all the way to the final two pieces. These were called "Liberation" and "V-J Day." Max leaned forward in his walker to touch the images with his fingers. It was as if he were returning to his youth, when he was only twenty, full of spit and vigor, ready to fight in a war that was killing his people and threatening his country.

As they departed the ramp, Sam and his father turned to view the "Freedom Wall," which held 4,048 gold stars, each representing a hundred Americans who died in the war. As they approached the Wall, Sam read the inscription, "Here we mark the price of freedom." Sam glanced down toward his father. He wasn't sure what his father was thinking at that moment as he looked at the Wall.

Sam often wondered how his dad must have felt surviving the war when many of his friends did not. How much pressure had he felt to make his life meaningful—since he had lived while others perished? Maybe that was why he chose to visit the Memorial.

Nearby, a large white tent had been erected for the hundred or so who came to the event. The tent was placed at the southern end of the fountain area, below the engravings that marked the Pacific theatre, and listed the battles fought in Guam, the Philippines, Manila, and finally, Iwo Jima and Okinawa.

At the reception table stood a naval officer. When Max introduced himself, the man responded with a salute and a firm handshake. He then walked Sam and his father to an area where other families had gathered to await the ceremony. The officer handed his father a pamphlet with the program's agenda and a list of honored attendees at the event. As Sam walked with his father to his seat, he saw a giant movie screen beside the lectern. After his dad sat down, Sam looked around. He recognized by their appearance that maybe forty or fifty in the crowd were likely veterans of the war and the rest were either family members or caregivers. Indeed, the crowd comprised not only the last living men from his father's ship, but also most of the last living American survivors of the Second World War. They were the last of the Greatest Generation.

As Max sat in his chair, he nodded as a friendly gesture to the other elderly men that sat around him, uncertain if, all these years later, he actually would remember any of them. Of the over two thousand men on the ship, it was like expecting a college student to know every other student at their school at a seventy-year reunion.

Max shifted his glasses to begin reading the program. Sam watched as his father scanned the names of the men lost on May 11th, 1945, assuming those had been men that his father knew. Maybe they had even been his closest friends. His father's fingers shook as his hand moved up and down the list quickly but carefully until he landed on one name. At that moment, piped-in music began to play, and those still standing found their seats.

The officer who had escorted Max to his seat approached the lectern and spoke. "My name is Captain Keith Barker. It is truly an honor to be here today. For those of you I have not met previously, my father was on the Bunker Hill. He was an aide to Admiral Marc Mitscher, commander of Task Force Fifty-Eight, which, as you all know, was led by the Bunker Hill. I invite you to sit back and watch this film with me."

The black-and-white film went on for about fifteen minutes. Although the timeline led to the remarkable events that transpired on May 11th, 1945, the film shared the unique history of the Bunker Hill during its three years of active commission. The film began with the ship's role during the invasion of the Gilbert Islands in 1943. It went on to cover the invasion of the Marshall Islands and the ship's air raid support during the attack on the Marianas and Palau Islands. The film also explained the Bunker Hill's place in the historic Battle of the Philippine Sea, where two sailors were killed and eighty more were wounded by scattered shrapnel during the first aerial bomb attack on the ship.

As the film ended, Captain Barker rose and approached the lectern, and he began to speak about May 11th, 1945. Now, static black-and-white pictures of the Bunker Hill appeared on the white screen. The first picture, taken from a nearby rescue ship, featured a billowing mass of black smoke emanating from the flight deck of the wounded carrier. Other images showed men running like ants along the deck, many toward the fires to douse them, and others running from them, either injured or carrying those injured.

Sam was mesmerized by the film and the photos, the captain's voice sharing the story of that fateful day. As Max studied the images, he retreated to his memories of the morning itself. The truth of that experience came rushing back and jolted him like a bolt of lightning.

Chapter 46

I T WAS ABOUT ten o'clock in the morning. Max was watching his monitor inside the CIC when suddenly, without warning, there was a sharp explosion. The impact shook the ship like a plate of jelly. Max realized they had been hit but was unsure of the magnitude of the damage. The lights flickered but stayed on, and a report was broadcast from the speaker above his head. The voice reported, "We are hit, port side aft."

That was the last understandable vocabulary Max heard that day in the Combatant Information Center since, within seconds, all hell broke loose as the ship suffered another hit. This explosion was closer and threw everyone in the CIC to the floor. The plane that hit the ship and the bomb attached to it had blown through its port side and torn the CIC to shambles. The lights went out, and strangling fumes of cordite and smoke filled the room. It was clear that the whole port side of the ship was on fire, and the screams of the wounded made the shock of the explosion even worse. Max lifted himself from the floor and understood in that instant that although he was somehow still alive, with the thickening smoke and fire around him, death was just a few moments away. The eerie gong of the general alarm mixed with the sounds of chaos from the men who had also survived in the CIC.

Max knew how the sailors had died on the Arizona and the Oklahoma during the attack on Pearl Harbor. Men like him who were below deck when the ships were hit drowned as they capsized where they were anchored. To survive, he needed to find his way out of the CIC and onto the deck. His lungs were starting to burn.

He stumbled around in the CIC in complete darkness, confused with shock. He felt a buzzing in his ears and the continued noise of the general alarm. It seemed like an eternity in darkness when Max saw light through the thick smoke. It came from an open hatch one deck above the one he was on. It was like an answer to his prayers. He needed to reach the opening. All that separated him from the needed oxygen was a metal chain ladder dangling from the hatch.

Max felt searing pain as he reached for each rung. Within seconds, he realized that he was burning his hands from the intensity of the heat on the metal ladder. But he had no other choice. He must have been in shock or so desperate for air that he didn't care. Then, while frozen on the ladder, he felt someone grab his collar and start pulling him up. He felt the temperature change as he went from below deck through the upper hatch.

Acrid smoke still filled the air as fires continued to burn below deck despite the efforts of those who had grabbed fire hoses to blanket the decks with water. Once on deck, he was lifted and carried away from the fires.

"Keep moving," Max heard the men with hoses yell. "Go toward the bow. Keep moving." He was fighting unconsciousness as he looked up and back at the fires behind him. The bow had been left intact. Someone was carrying him to safety.

Nearby, destroyers and other vessels sprayed the ship with water to help contain the fires. Somehow, any ammunition that the fires had not already triggered lay quiet. If the fires had reached further fuel depots or the lines of bombs that stood ready for the planes, there would have been little left of the vessel, but the kamikazes and their weapons had somehow missed the heart of the ship. As the fires quieted, the surviving crew began to understand that their vessel would not sink. It was badly damaged, but it was still floating.

Max felt himself being moved from one person to another until he was placed on a stretcher. He could hear the ongoing bombardment of Okinawa and the sound of planes sweeping above him. He was being saved, but the battle raged on.

Chapter 47

C APTAIN BARKER CONTINUED to advance picture after picture of the Bunker Hill as it burned, photos taken from adjacent ships as the water hoses from the other ships were turned to try to save the burning carrier.

Although Sam had seen the pictures of the Bunker Hill over the years, he had never taken the time to really study what happened to the ship during the infamous battles of Okinawa. And whatever he had seen did not seem real, but instead like abstract images from a movie starring John Wayne or Tom Hanks. Now, though, as he saw these images on the screen, he began to understand this event's significance in his father's life. His father was only twenty years old when it happened. The tension, fear, death, and pain had all been real for him.

Sam watched each photo and then turned to watch his dad. Tears were welling in his father's eyes. He could not bear to see his dad in such pain. But he held back from speaking.

This was a side of the man that he didn't know. Sam had never talked to his father in detail about the war. It was a part of his father that had been locked away for years. Finally, 70 years later, Max allowed himself to re-enter the time. Sam couldn't even imagine what his father was feeling.

When Captain Barker finished his presentation, he invited one of Max's fellow crew members to address the attendees. The elderly gentleman rose and approached the lectern slowly, gathering his composure before speaking. The microphone picked up his feeble voice.

"My name is Lawrence Garrett. I was a third mate stationed onboard the Bunker Hill from 1942 through 1945. On May 11, the admiral ordered the air squadrons to begin their daily assault on the island. I was on the flight deck when the kamikazes hit our ship. It was mid-morning. The first Japanese Zero broke through the anti-aircraft screen and released its bomb just above the flight deck. The plane crashed into the fully fueled planes waiting on the deck. The munitions and gasoline exploded and knocked us all back. Fire engulfed the fight deck and spread across the back of the carrier. There was smoke and fire everywhere on the ship."

The man continued with his story.

"I was lucky. Below me, in the hanger bay, so many were killed by the bomb's explosion. Black smoke was pouring from the inside of the ship as the fire combined with the gasoline for the planes. The smell of burning flesh was overwhelming. It was horrible. Then, not a minute later, a second kamikaze plane hit the ship with another bomb, crashing near the tower and the ready room. When that bomb hit, it killed another hundred men. But men remained at their stations, putting out the fires and performing rescues. The wounded gathered at the bow at the part of the flight deck farthest from the damage. The men had organized a makeshift first aid station. Those who were able continued to battle to put out the flames. Others stayed at their anti-aircraft stations to challenge the remaining Japanese planes as they continued their attack."

The man's voice quivered as he spoke. He looked down. He had no script. He was reliving the experience as he told the story.

"Through the bombing, fire, explosions, and chaos, our guns remained in action. There was a third Jap plane that made its dive at us. Our guns blasted away at the target as it approached. I remember men cheering, 'The bastard's hit, he's going down!' when they hit the target. Those men saved our ship. At least momentarily, we didn't have to worry about another bomb. I remember looking back at the section of the ship that was on fire. All seemed ablaze, with the crew working like mad trying to control it. A cruiser and a destroyer were on each side of us, giving every possible assistance. Finally, after what seemed like forever, the word passed that the fires were under control."

He paused and looked up to the audience. The group was mesmerized by the story that had just been shared.

"Our ship was saved by the heroic efforts of the officers and men who refused to give the Bunker Hill up to a watery grave. And the men of the Bunker Hill and its families are the beneficiaries of that sacrifice."

The man bowed his head and then returned to his seat.

Captain Barker rose again to thank Mr. Garrett for his words, then introduced a Navy chaplain to guide the group through a moment of silence for the fallen and to present a benediction to conclude the service. A small military band ensemble began to play "Taps." As the music began, Sam felt Max shift in his seat. Then Max, pushing against his walker, rose to attention.

Others in the group followed, standing at attention as the music played on. The shrill call of the bugle was chilling after having just re-lived the event through the pictures. Sam stood with his dad. It was a somber moment, one that made Sam tremble a bit to try to understand what his dad might be feeling.

As Max heard the bugle, his memory flashed to the massive burial at sea that he had witnessed. He saw the images of the wrapped bodies that spilled from each American-flag-draped stretcher as they were lifted and tilted toward the sea from the side of the ship's deck. The bodies were released into the Pacific Ocean as the names were spoken. Too many were lost to keep on the carrier and return to shore.

Now, he looked toward the flags flying inside the World War II Memorial. He had been one of the injured. He had been burned by the fires and while climbing the metal ladder, but doctors on the ship treated him, and he was saved.

He and others stayed with the ship as it crawled back, badly damaged, to return to Pearl Harbor. By June 1945, he would be back home in New York. The war would soon be over.

Chapter 48

SAM TOOK A moment to try to comprehend his father's experience from seventy years ago. The words and pictures could not do justice to the life experience. Sam closed his eyes to picture his father as a young man suffering for survival. He imagined the sound and sense of the bombs, the smell, the darkness, and the fear consuming the men around him—all looking for a way to escape, all looking for air. To breathe. All he could do was try to imagine the experience. He could only see it in his head as a dramatization—as if he were watching his father through a screen, as he would for any television show or movie. He was experiencing everything as a third-party witness.

The images in Sam's mind swirled as he considered his father's effort to survive. That young man who would one day be his father had battled for his life, plain and simple. The location of the bomb's explosion, whether the hatch opened, and whether the ship stayed afloat—all these things determined his father's survival—and but for his survival that day, Sam would not even be here.

Sam couldn't help but be emotional. Thoughts blasted through his head about his father's life and his own. He accepted that his father had faced war as a young man. But he also realized that his father had faced many battles in his ninety years. He had managed a marriage, a career, and a family. During those ninety years, he had lost a son and his wife. The economy had gone up, but it had also gone down. His business had survived. Max had lived a life of battles.

Sam then thought of his own life. Sam appreciated that he never had to go to war, but in his sixty years, he had seen his own battles. He saw himself in a fight every day to win, to survive. He knew he was luckier than most. He had won most of his battles, and things were still okay. Standing there with his father, he knew that he would endure more battles before it was over, maybe even a battle over cancer. But for the first time, Sam began to recognize that the battle was just life itself. Every day presented new challenges, and he had made it through so far. He thought about the things that his father had said to him. That "life is a battle, but worth the fight." He was starting to understand it a bit more.

Chapter 49

THERE WAS SILENCE on the way back from the reunion. Sam was so tempted to talk with his father, but he knew better than to ask any questions now. Instead, they checked into the hotel Lynn had reserved and crashed on their beds. It was already after six o'clock. Max had spent a good amount of time after the program talking with Mr. Garrett, Captain Barker, and others who had gathered together after the benediction.

"I'll grab us some dinner and come back," Sam said. "How does that sound?"

"That would be nice," his father answered, still distant from the events of the day.

"Anything special you want, Dad?"

"I'm fine with anything. Just tired."

"I'm going to take a quick shower to wake up," Sam said. He grabbed some clothes and toiletries from his suitcase and went into the bathroom.

When he emerged, his father was asleep. His shoes were still on. Sam decided to let him rest. He quietly left the room to find some food.

Lynn had found them a room in Crystal City, just a few miles from the heart of DC. The rates were better, and they were within walking distance of several shops and restaurants that had sprung up in the last decade. Sam could not get over the area's growth since he had last been in DC.

As he walked, he pulled out his phone and dialed his daughter. It was still early on a Saturday night.

"Dad?" The sound of his daughter's voice was reassuring. "Everything okay?'

"Yes. Yes," Sam said. "I was thinking about you and Aaron. You both would have been very proud of Grandpa today."

"You still with Grandpa?" she asked.

"Yes. He's asleep in the hotel room. We're right outside of DC. We'll head home tomorrow. It was a pretty emotional day to hear about Grandpa's experiences during World War II. There's a lot to the story. Such a tragedy."

His daughter could hear the stress in her father's voice. "You okay, Dad?"

Sam had a special bond with his daughter. Lucy understood his weak side. It helped any time she wanted something. He couldn't say no to her. But she also knew when he was sad. He couldn't hide it from her. He had a different connection with Aaron. It was less emotional and more practical, even though Sam often wanted more. Sam always understood that there was a difference between daughters and sons, at least with his kids.

Sam hesitated to speak honestly with his daughter. He loved her too much to worry her. He wanted to tell her about his father's nightmares or that he was worried about his own health and his upcoming diagnosis. He wanted to tell her that life was short and to try to be happy. He wanted to warn her about the evil in the world and the challenges that lay ahead of her.

Instead, he simply said "I'm fine. Grandpa's fine. This has been a great trip."

He knew that he was being over-protective, but he also believed that it was not her job to worry about her parents or her grandparents.

"Thanks for listening, sweetheart. Have a good night. Will I see you when I get back to town?"

"Maybe," she said. "I thought I might take a week off before my internship starts. Go to the mountains with some friends."

"Sounds like fun. I love you."

"Love you, too, Dad."

Sam was about to call Lynn next but hesitated when he saw a

burger place. It was someplace he could order dinner for them and grab a beer while he waited.

Max was awake and watching TV when Sam returned to the room.

"Good to see you up. I was wondering if I would have to eat your burger, too!" Sam said.

The men settled over the table in the room and enjoyed their food. Both were hungry.

"I spoke to Lucy tonight. She told me that she was proud of you."

"For what?" his father asked.

"For your service," Sam quickly answered.

"How about Aaron? Have you talked to him, too?"

"No. Not yet."

Sam was silent. It had already been an emotional day.

"Are you two okay?" his father asked.

Sam hesitated further. It was not an easy question for him to answer. "Honestly, I don't know, Dad. He's living his own life."

"What does that mean?"

"I worry about him," Sam explained, "I can't help it." Then he confessed to his father "I think I put too much pressure on him."

"How?" His father asked.

"I'm not sure. I'm probably just worried that I've set high expectations for him."

"You just want him to succeed."

"But Dad, it's stressful. A life built around expectations and the risk of failure. It's a hard mountain to climb, easy to fall."

"Did I put that on you?" his dad asked.

"Not directly. But I worked the way I did to make you proud. To make Mom proud. I wanted you to feel that all of your sacrifices were worth it."

"Son, I never demanded anything. You just took it upon yourself."

"Yes. You expected things of Ben and me, yes. But you were a pushover compared to some of my friends' dads." Sam laughed.

"So, why is that different with Aaron? You don't make demands. He has his own goals."

"I know, I know. But I still blame myself."

"He'll be fine. Did I ever tell you that you're a worrier?" his dad asked.

"I get that from Mom, right?" He knew the answer.

"Yes, you do."

"Are you telling me that there was a time when you stopped worrying about Ben and me?" He'd had asked the question without thinking through the obvious discomfort he created by mentioning Ben.

"No, you're right. I worried about you boys all the time."

Sam didn't know what to say. Ben had not made it. The sadness hung in Sam's brain any time he spoke to his dad about his brother.

"You and Ben were always different," said Max, seeing the conflict in Sam's face. "I can't explain it. Same parents, same upbringing, different paths, different stories."

Sam always thought that he had benefitted from being the youngest. He'd had the chance to watch his brother—and learn what worked and what didn't. Now, he couldn't help but connect his angst about Ben with his angst about Aaron.

"I know that you are worried about him, "his father said. All parents worry about their children. Just give it time."

"Really?" Sam asked, hoping that his father would be right.

The ninety-year old man reached over and grabbed the top of his son's hand.

"Yes. Really" Max said.

"It's all okay, Dad," he said. "Thanks for listening."

"And thanks for the burger, son." His father smiled.

It didn't take long for either of them to call it a night and get into bed. Sam was expecting a long drive home in the morning.

After his dad had gone to sleep, he texted Lynn. He said he would tell her the whole story once he got home. She replied with an emoji heart.

Settling into his own bed, he took his phone and typed "Bunker Hill, World War II" into Google. Up flashed some of the photos he had seen today. Sam read, "On May 11th, 1945, the Bunker Hill was attacked by two kamikaze attack aircraft – the first released a 550-pound bomb that tore through the ship and exploded in the sea before the plane struck flight deck. Thirty seconds later, another plane repeated the same attack, releasing a similar bomb, which exploded in the ship's interior near the pilots' ready room. Three hundred and ninety three men aboard the Bunker Hill were killed or never found, and two hundred and sixty-four men were wounded in the attack."

Sam looked at the pictures, at the fires and the bodies stacked atop one another as the men fought to escape from below deck. Trapped by the explosion with nowhere to go, they fought in vain to survive. Most died from asphyxiation before the fires claimed their bodies.

He looked again at the numbers. Of the three hundred and ninety-three sailors and airmen that were killed, forty-one were never found. There were 264 men like his dad who were injured in the attacks. But it was the pictures of the burials at sea that made Sam's heart sink. The men who died and were recovered were buried at sea. As he continued reading, he understood that it was the longest burial-at-sea ceremony in the history of the US Navy. He tried to comprehend the enormity of what had happened that day.

Then Sam typed in "Okinawa." By most accounts, the Battle of Okinawa was one of the bloodiest of the war in the Pacific, with the most casualties. The article said that more than 160,000 men were killed over three months, including civilians on the island who'd been conscripted to fight for the Japanese. The battle was called the "Rain of Steel" because of the number of ships involved in the Allied armada and the intensity of kamikaze attacks—which the Japanese had increased due to frustration over Allied movement in the Pacific and the fear that Allied forces would invade the Japanese homeland. Sam read that the battle would continue to be fought until June 22nd, 1945, over a month and a half after the Bunker Hill attack. It would be one of the most protracted of World War II, lasting almost three months.

Sam went on to read about the ship's war record. His father's ship had participated in every major invasion in the Pacific War, from the Marshall Islands to Okinawa. The ship's artillery and aircraft had damaged more than 450,000 tons of enemy ships, downed 470 enemy aircraft, and sunk more than 400,000 tons of enemy ships. The Bunker Hill was also considered the most seriously damaged warship to return from the war. It lived up to its motto, "Never surrender, never sink," even though the ship never returned to combat. Instead, years later, it was sold as scrap. Sam then recalled that his father had written his senators pleading to save the ship when it was scheduled to be dismantled. His father was distraught that no one would listen. Sam tried to imagine how his father must have felt when he could no longer defend the ship from its destruction, and Sam thought about the men who had fought and died to protect it during the war. It bothered Sam that after all the death and despair, the ship was treated as scrap. There was a lesson in that story somewhere. It wasn't a good one.

Before he went to sleep, Sam texted Aaron about the ceremony. He just wanted to reach out. He didn't expect a reply. He didn't get one.

Chapter 50

A S LUCY HUNG up the phone with her father, worry washed over her. Her dad sounded stressed. He was a man who wore his heart on his sleeve. No matter how much he kept his emotions in check, she always knew what was going on. She could hear it in his questions and the tidbits he offered. He never shared his worries with them, except those for their safety. He always wanted them to check in to ensure they were okay. And his questions always went to the heart of whether they were happy.

She knew that this trip with his father would not be easy. She knew Grandpa had gotten weaker over the last few years without her grandmother and as the years took their toll.

Lucy was a pleaser. She wanted everyone around her to be happy. Maybe it was because she was the baby in the family or because she was the daughter, but she tried to keep peace and avoid trouble. She didn't complain when they moved from New York to Nashville after she graduated from middle school. Her parents had told her she would make new friends just in time for high school.

She understood her brother and why he never came back after college. He didn't want to live with them in Nashville. Lucy, on the other hand, found comfort in Nashville. She loved her time in college and was enjoying graduate school but longed to return.

She never admitted it, but she envied what her grandparents and her parents had created for themselves over the years in Nashville. A good life. Simple but fulfilling. And there was a lot of love to tie it all together. She hoped for the same in her future.

Lucy also believed that when she returned with her degree that she could build a strong practice in Nashville. She would have an impact in her community. She would make a difference.

She hadn't met the right guy yet, but she knew what she was looking for. If nothing else, it would ultimately have to be someone her parents approved of. It was part of the deal. He would have to love her family, and they would have to love him. She knew there would be no other way.

She sent her dad a text. "Love you. Big hugs to Grandpa, too".

Aaron had seen the text from his father that night. He hesitated and decided not to reply. He would call back after his dad and grandfather got home from their trip. It wasn't that he didn't care. He struggled with how easy it would be just to stop what he was doing and go back home. But Nashville didn't offer him the same opportunities as New York. He loved his family, but to Aaron, going back was stepping back. He thought of his uncle and how he had ended up back in Nashville. Going home had been a dead end for him; Aaron wanted more. So, he had to move forward even if he left his family behind. He wanted to prove something not only to them but to himself. He thought about his grandfather. He had left New York to start his own life. Even his dad had left Nashville to go to work in New York. Maybe one day he would come home too, but not yet.

Chapter 51

WHEN THE SUNRISE peeked through the hotel room shades, Sam realized it was his sign to start moving and get ready for the trip back to Nashville. He knew he'd be able to handle making the drive in a day, but whether that actually happened depended on his dad and how he was feeling.

Max stirred in the bed.

Sam realized that the earlier they left DC, the better chance they had of making it home by the evening. Then, he could be back in the office on Monday. He looked at his watch. It was only 7:30. Too early to wake his dad. He calculated that they would need to be on the road by ten o'clock at the latest to reasonably have a chance to drive straight through. He quietly slipped on his jeans, a t-shirt, and shoes and left the room. He decided to go down to the lobby, read the Sunday *New York Times*, and grab some coffee. By the time Sam returned to the room with a large coffee for his father, his dad was up and showered. He was sitting in his boxers with a towel around his shoulders. He looked to be resting before he tried to get dressed.

"Wow. I expected you to sleep all morning," Sam said.

"No. Too much on my mind. Enough sleep."

"Okay. Do you want to have breakfast here or on the road? I was thinking we could make it back to Nashville tonight..."

His father looked up from the bed and interrupted Sam mid-sentence. "Sam, we need to go to Arlington Cemetery this morning."

"Arlington? Why?"

"It's another part of why I wanted to make the trip here. I need to see someone."

Sam worked a bit to understand what his dad meant by "seeing" someone. "Is it even open?" he asked.

"Yes. Later this morning. It won't take long, but it's important."

Sam realized that any stop like that would blow their chances of making it back to Nashville tonight. But again, he didn't have the heart to question his dad. He would keep their reservations at the hotel in Knoxville that Lynn had originally made for them. They would hopefully make it there in time for dinner. The logistics streamed through his head. He would need to let his office know that he would not be back now until Tuesday. His head was spinning with how he would manage being gone from work for the additional day.

"Dad. Can you tell me who we're seeing? It's a big place. Do you know how to find the marker?"

"The office is open at eleven. They'll help us."

Again, even though Sam was confident that there was technology online that would likely give them the information they needed, Sam was willing to defer to his father and go "old school." Well, they had come this far. Another adventure was just par for the course. "Okay, Dad. Why don't you finish getting ready? Then I'll jump in the shower. We'll hit the road and go to the cemetery. I've actually always wanted to see the Kennedy eternal light."

"Him, I voted for!" his dad exclaimed. "They never should have elected Nixon. He was a crook." And he got up and closed the bathroom door.

Sam shook his head. At this pace, he wasn't even sure they would make it to Knoxville tonight. Sam wasn't happy. He felt the rise in his blood pressure about this additional delay.

After breakfast, Max waited in the lobby as Sam gathered the luggage and swung the car around front to pick up his dad.

The drive to Arlington took less than fifteen minutes. As they parked the car in front of the information office, his father leaned over to Sam and whispered, "This is who I need to find today." He handed him the program from the reunion with a name circled on the list of those lost on May eleventh: "Tony Carletto."

As Max had hoped, the information center provided them with a map and clear directions to the marker.

It took them about five minutes of driving through the different sections of the cemetery before they found the right area. The perfect geometry of the landscape was overwhelming to see. The markers seemed to go on forever. As the sun rose higher and the clouds broke, the light bounced off of the whiteness of the individual headstones, and the area glowed.

Sam parked as close as he could to where he knew the stone would be. He helped his father from the car and handed him his walker. They had to navigate themselves to find the right row and column. The stone was now only fifteen or twenty feet away. He and his father approached the area slowly.

As they got closer, Sam stood back as his father continued and slowly shifted his walker across the grass to approach the white marker. From where he stood, Sam could see the faint outline of Tony's name, as well as the date. May 11, 1945.

As he reached the gravestone, Max leaned forward and touched the top of the white stone with his hand. He then grasped onto the structure as if he was holding on for his life. Sam noticed his father's hand cast a shade of blue as blood circulation struggled to flow through the clasped hand. Max talked to the marker as if involved in a profound conversation. It only lasted a moment or two, but it seemed longer. Then, Max released his grip on the stone, straightened his posture, and removed a chain from over his neck. It was his military dog tags. Max gathered the tags in his hands and placed them on the white stone.

It was hard for Sam to watch this personal exchange: his father seemingly negotiating a deal with a ghost. But Tony must have been alive in his dad's mind. It otherwise seemed too real to disregard. Was it an apology? An offer of forgiveness? An overdue thank-you? Or an admonishment for something that happened that day?

Whatever it was, his father turned back toward Sam, and Sam

saw tears form again in his dad's eyes. Before this weekend, he had only really seen his father cry twice, once at his mother's funeral and again at Ben's funeral. Clearly, this was something his dad had needed to do for years. Sam felt good that he was helping his dad accomplish so much closure during this trip.

When Max returned to where Sam was standing, he said, "Tony was my best friend. We came from different places, but we were the same. We both knew the risks. I made it home alive, and he didn't."

"Sorry, Dad. I didn't know." Sam was trying to apologize to his father.

"We had talked about him being my best man at our wedding. He really wanted to meet your mom. He didn't understand why I didn't chase skirts when we had our leave. He was quite a character."

"Did you ever meet his family after the war?" Sam asked.

"I always wanted to but never did. They shipped me back to Pearl Harbor and then to Washington state to recover from my burns. While I was in the hospital, they dropped the A-bombs. The war was over. I wanted to leave it all behind me. I went back to New York. Your mom and I got married." His paused. "I had been given a chance to live, so I never looked back. It was too hard."

"Why now, Dad?"

"You reach a point in life, son, when you have to accept what you have done and what others have done to you. There is no carry-over. You have to make amends with the time you have. Life is life. Good and bad. I have made peace with your mom, your brother, and now this last piece of my life."

"Dad, you still have time."

"For what, Sam? I have lived my life. I loved. I built. I shared. Time for the next generation to follow." Sam felt himself shudder. He was the next generation. But he wasn't ready.

As they drove from the cemetery, Sam couldn't help but think about the loss that his father had experienced during his life. First in the war, then losing his mom, and then Ben.

But through it all, Max had kept a positive spirit that made others feel comfortable around him. He did not collapse from the weight of the despair. He told others that everything was all right. At first, Sam had not understood how his father could cope with such loss. Now he was starting to see: For his father, each of these experiences was just another of life's battles.

Maybe, Sam thought, it was from the war that his father had built the strength to manage it. For years, he hadn't understood how his father had handled it. The demons of losing his mother and brother weighed heavily on Sam. He felt betrayed; cheated. He was the one without a mother. He was the one who had lost a brother.

He knew he was good at hiding things. He called it "compartmentalizing" his life. Work was work, and home was home. Whatever he felt as he ground through work every day stopped at the threshold of his house. Or at least that is what he tried to do. Many days he realized that he moped around the house, reflecting on the stress and issues from work as he tried to keep his happy face at home.

Similarly, whenever things were tough at home, with Lynn, the kids, or making ends meet, he had no choice but to put it aside when he went to the office. His clients did not care for a minute about his other problems. They wanted their work done; their problem solved first. That's why they were paying him. On a purely rational level, Sam understood this. So, he turned off that side of his brain to focus on work as his problems at home continued. Sam could not face spinning two sets of plates at once. He couldn't do both. He didn't have it in him. Without separating his battlefields, he would lose both.

Sam had always admired his dad for seamlessly managing his home and work life. Or so he assumed. As Sam got older, he realized that his dad had just learned to balance the two, just as he did. And as the realization grew that his dad had not been perfect, the pressure waned for Sam. But it never went away. It was too ingrained just to let go. Each day Sam opened one door and closed another, and he did that for a long, long time. Sam was growing tired of playing those games.

Sam was scared about his potential cancer, scared about his children's future, and scared about his life in the future. He still needed his dad. It gave him comfort and a psychological safety net knowing that he was there for him. At least for now.

Chapter 52

AFTER THEY LEFT from Arlington, it was a quiet drive from DC to Knoxville. It was about seven o'clock Sunday night when Sam and Max finally pulled into the hotel in Knoxville. They discussed that they would finish their trip in the morning and hopefully be home in the afternoon.

"Dad, no more surprises, right?" Sam would say, trying to explain to his dad that he had to eventually get back to his office.

"Yes," his father would say. But Sam was not convinced.

After they brought their bags up to the room and washed up, they decided to go to the bar in the lobby and have a drink. Neither one of them was hungry after snacking during most of the drive.

They sat at the bar: just a father and a son.

"Two bourbons, neat, please. Woodford if you have it," said Sam.

The two men toasted with their glasses and took a long sip.

Max said, "L'chaim, to life!" Sam smiled back at his father, recognizing the "Fiddler" reference.

"Quite a trip, Dad. Quite a trip." Sam said.

"Sam. Thank you for taking me." His father said, his gaze on his son.

Sam took another sip from his glass and turned back to his father. "Dad. Will you finish the story for me? What happened after the attack? What happened to you?"

Max reflected on the moment, staring into his drink. After the film and photos he had seen the day before, the images were more vibrant in his mind than they had been in years. He began to talk.

"After the bomb went off, I was in the dark. The smoke was thick and smelled like poison. I couldn't breathe. I thought I was going to die by suffocating. Then I saw light from a hatch and then the chain ladder. I started to climb the ladder. It was on fire. My hands were burning."

"Dad. How did you get out?"

Sam watched his father's head settle as if a weight were being lifted. "It was Tony. He came back to save me. He was the one that carried me to the bow. Then he went back to his gun station"

"Tony? Tony was the one that got you out?"

Sam asked "He's the one that pulled you from the ladder?"

"Yes." His father's words were soft. "After we were hit, he came looking for me. He knew that the CIC had been hit. He came to find me."

Sam stopped to think about the level of friendship the two men must have had during their short time on the ship together.

"I was covered in blood. My hands were burned. He carried me to the bow of the ship, where the first aid area had been set up. Then he went back to the fight."

Sam did not interrupt. He watched his father as he continued with his story. The story hypnotized Sam.

"I was given morphine. A chaplain passed by, asked how I was doing, and said something comforting. He didn't know I was Jewish. It didn't matter. I was scared. I kept wondering, what would I do if we had to abandon ship? With my hands such a mess, I would drown. Time passed, and all I could see were men rushing here and there, shouting orders. A pilot asked me if I wanted a smoke, and when I showed him my bandaged hands and arms, he leaned over, put a cigarette to my lips, lit it, and stood by while I took a few drags. This all seemed like an eternity, but I know it happened in just a few minutes."

Sam hesitated, but he had to ask.

"Dad. What about Tony? The man you went to visit today?"

Max sat stoically for a minute. Then he looked into his son's eyes.

"There were witnesses who said he managed to make his way

back to the fifty-millimeter guns. It was Tony who shot down that third plane. He saved me and hundreds more of us who were on the ship that day. None of us would have survived if the third plane had hit us."

The Max said, "He died from aircraft fire less than thirty minutes later."

"Dad. I'm so sorry" Sam said. His hand reaching for his father's shoulder.

"He received a posthumous medal of valor." His dad continued. "Tony was my best friend on the ship. He was a great friend. But I wouldn't be here today if it hadn't been for him. I made it out. He didn't." His father took a drink of his bourbon and began to whisper. "There were so many killed that day. Some were burned beyond recognition. They were just ash. They should have been able to read the dog tags, but sometimes, they couldn't find them. They were trying to find their names on their belts or jackets, where some had stenciled them. Eventually, they identified them by their dental records. Some died from the blasts, others from the fire or the smoke. There were hundreds of bodies, and we were a thousand miles from home. They had no choice but to bury them at sea. I watched."

His father took another sip from his drink, another pause.

"They used canvas on the ship to make the shrouds. In each bag, they put the body and two five-inch artillery shells, each weighing fifty pounds. One was tied around the chest, and the other around the legs. They released six bodies at once. It took eight hours. A rabbi, a Protestant minister, or a Catholic priest would say a prayer depending on the religion of the deceased. There was no sound other than the prayers. Three hundred and fifty-two men were buried that day."

Max was looking down. His vision went beyond the drink in his hand and into the past. His mind's eye could see the canvas bags, the American flags flapping in the wind, the sound of taps, and the twenty-one-gun salute--each shot from the gun a piercing blast. His dad squirmed a bit in his chair and did not look up.

"I prayed that morning during the attack," he began. "I prayed for my own life and the ship's survival."

"You think God answered your prayers?" Sam asked.

"I'm here, aren't I?" He lifted his head and looked again at his son.

Sam felt a sort of spiritual pain in his heart. His father had faith. Again, why didn't Sam? At that moment, Sam wanted to tell his dad about his test results and his impending biopsy. And that Sam wanted to have faith as well.

His father's voice quivered as he spoke.

"It was the only time I really prayed other than when your mom was dying. I just couldn't imagine living without her. I don't know how to explain it. Everything changed when your mom died. But then I eventually accepted that death is a part of life." His father reached out and took hold of his son's shoulder. "Sam, I know it's scary. But it's okay. When my time comes, I'll find peace knowing I did my part. Your mom and I loved you and Ben so much. It is time for you to have your life and raise your kids. I did it without my mom and dad. You can do it without Mom and me."

"Dad. Don't talk like that."

"Sam, I remember a story where someone was asked whether they would want to live forever – but in exchange, no new lives would happen. Can you imagine no new babies? Life without Lucy and Aaron, my wonderful grandchildren? It would be selfish to say that I want to live forever. Although I will so miss seeing you and watching my grandchildren grow up."

Sam looked for the waitress. He wanted to pay their tab. The conversation was hard to hear. He knew the words were honest. But, after the last few days, it was more than he could handle.

They spoke no other words that night. Max got into bed and closed his eyes. Sam lay in his bed, still fully dressed, and opened his laptop, scanning his e-mails and some news sites. Then he lay awake, thinking about his dad and the life he was able to create after the war, returning to Brooklyn to marry his mother.

Sam remembered gathering in the house after his mom's funeral for the shiva. They all sat in the formal living room looking at family photo albums. Ben was sitting on the couch next to his dad.

"Finally, we get to use this formal living room," Ben had said, repeating the family joke for years about how his mother had kept this one room closed to visitors.

"Only for special occasions," Sam had said. "She didn't want any of us in here otherwise. She didn't trust us." His father called the room her "showpiece."

At one point, Ben had said, "Hey, Dad. You should look at the other side of that cushion. I think I spilled a drink there a long time ago."

Sam remembered them all laughing, especially his father.

But his father never used the room again. It had been Rose's living room.

Chapter 53

MAX WAS SOUND asleep. Sam could not fall asleep no matter what he did. He had not brought any Ambien with him because he'd thought he should stay alert while traveling with his dad.

Finally, he gave up, quietly grabbing his pants and his shoes before opening the door to their room.

It was after 11:00. Only after pressing the button to call his wife and bringing his phone to his ear did the events from the last few days cascade over him.

"Hi, honey," she answered. "Where are you?"

"Knoxville. We spent the morning at Arlington Cemetery but only made it part of the way home. We'll be there tomorrow."

"You want to stop by and say hi to my folks?" Lynn asked.

"Maybe the next trip. My dad is more than I can handle on this trip!" Sam said to his wife.

"How's your dad?"

"Okay, I think. He's asleep now. He was exhausted." Sam released a deep breath.

"Sounds like you had a long day."

"A long weekend. I'd had no idea what he experienced in the war."

"Can you tell me?" she asked.

"Sure. But that's the thing. Words don't do it justice. It has given me a completely different perspective on what war is. What it means. How it can forever change you. Become a part of you. I don't think I ever appreciated any piece of that until I saw what I saw today and talked to my dad. It was the first time I ever heard him talk about it. I feel like I never really knew him. He had lived a whole other life before we became part of it."

"Other veterans were there?"

"About fifty people. A lot of family and caregivers. Not many are left or were able to travel. It was seventy years ago. That's a whole lifetime by itself. From my perspective, World War Two felt like the Civil War. Only a piece of history, nothing more. But my dad lived it. Felt it. Suffered it. I can't explain how important it all seems now. The war memorial does not do it justice."

"Wow. I can tell this was emotional for you. Are you okay?"

"Yes. But I can't just move on from this like it's nothing. His story and what happened need to be kept alive. At least in our family. His service cannot be forgotten. His life cannot be forgotten." Sam knew he was talking about his dad but realized that maybe, he was also talking about himself. He was feeling very fragile in the life department.

"I love you," he said. "I love our life."

"We're very lucky," Lynn said.

Tears welled up in Sam's eyes. "I know."

Chapter 54

IS DAD REALLY was now "ready" when his time came. That's what he'd said, but Sam didn't want to hear it, even though it was important to his father that he say it. He'd simply said, "I'm not afraid of dying."

The more time Sam spent with him, recognizing his growing frailty, the more he began to accept that he wouldn't live forever either.

He couldn't help but think about his mom. He always wondered how she had felt about getting sick. She'd never talked about it, just said she was doing "fine," all while fighting like a champ. Went to every doctor and took every treatment. When she realized there wasn't anything more they could do for her, she found peace in the joy of her life. Sam thought he saw anger in his dad like he had never witnessed in her.

But Sam tried to find the lesson from her ordeal. He thought about his doctor's visit and understood that a fight was coming for him. He wanted to be as strong as she was, or at least how she appeared to be.

Sam intellectually understood the limits of life. He had planned for it. He and Lynn had prepared their wills. They had a plan for the kids and charities they wanted to support. But it was one thing to plan for it and another to accept its reality. Then Sam smiled. He knew he still considered himself "young." He was active. He thought he could handle both the physical and mental obstacles before him. He thought, maybe on a good day, he was still how he felt in his forties. But it was all a mirage. He didn't want to think about it. Why should he? No one else seemed to.

Even though Sam was experiencing the fragility of life, he had so much to look forward to. He was thinking about the kids and how he wanted to be around for their life cycle experiences. Lynn and Sam were looking forward to Aaron and Lucy meeting their life partners and settling down. Maybe even the possibility of grandchildren one day. It all seemed so possible, even though right now, it seemed so far away. He wanted to be here for all of it. He would fight to be here.

Chapter 55

LATER THAT NIGHT, after his father fell asleep, Sam tossed and turned himself. As was so often the case, he thought about Ben and what had happened that night. The memory was as clear to him as if it had happened yesterday.

Ben wasn't answering his cell. It had been two, maybe three days of Sam trying to reach him. It wasn't unusual for Ben to ignore Sam's calls. But his dad had not heard from him either.

This time it was quiet. Too quiet. Even though it was a bit of a drive to get to where he lived, if Ben wasn't going to answer his calls, Sam would go there himself.

Sam was pissed. Another wave of irresponsible behavior. As Sam drove, he began to craft his words to chastise Ben for his actions. The last straw had been the collection calls. They had called for Ben at his house, and Lynn had answered. The debt collector's intimidation had scared her. Then the same company called his folks' house and told his father they would issue a warrant for Ben's arrest. Sam knew that they wouldn't do that. There weren't debtors' prisons, and Ben hadn't stolen anything. He just hadn't paid his bills, and they were chasing him to find some money. It was illegal to make such a threat and what made Sam angry was how upset his father had been after the call. Sam was going to end this. He was going to pay off Ben's debts. Maybe that would stop this for a while.

As he was driving to confront Ben, he was thinking about taking from his 401k to pay off Ben's debts. How he wanted to tell him just to go away and stop hurting the family! Sam was angry. Maybe, even more, he was disappointed in his brother. He knew it had been the liquor and the drugs that had caused the broken relationships, the anger, and the depression, but he believed it had all been self-inflicted. That Ben had a choice. Just like Sam did. Sam had crept close to the line with prescription drugs and too many scotches, but he had kept himself from going over. He didn't understand why his brother didn't have the same self-control.

But Sam also knew in his heart that maybe it was something else, possibly demons Ben couldn't control. Sam didn't want to accept that or believe in that possibility because he was afraid that if it were true for Ben, then it could be true for him. The demons. Maybe it was in their genes. Brothers are brothers. No matter what, Sam still loved his older brother.

The front door to Ben's apartment was partially open, and Ben was alone, sitting in his recliner and slumped over. The image would never leave Sam's memory. There were no needles. Sam assumed it had been pills and booze. He remembered dialing 911, the police lights, and the EMTs attending to Ben. The questions, the reports. He remembered having to tell his father that his eldest son was gone. It was so hard on his father, especially after losing his wife.

Every time Sam thought about Ben, he couldn't help but think about how young he had been when he died. He was only sixty, Sam's age now. He was way too young to die. Clearly, things had gotten rough for him. He had lost Trish, and then there had been a series of failed relationships. He had lost his job, and then Mom had died. But they all agreed that it must have been an accident, that Ben would not have intended to kill himself, no matter how bad things had gotten. Sam understood why Ben would have turned to drugs and alcohol. Yes, Ben used drugs, lots of them, and was always drinking. But Sam never thought of Ben as a drug addict or an alcoholic.

He realized now that he'd been kidding himself.

Sam had found comfort in the belief that when it happened, when Ben was dying, he would have been unconscious from the drugs. Sam hoped that Ben didn't realize that the final dose he had taken would kill him; otherwise, he worried that Ben would have been afraid.

Sam imagined the night that Ben died to be like others he had easily survived, a mixture of different drugs and too much alcohol. The only difference was that this time, he didn't wake up.

Sam thought about his dad. He couldn't imagine a world where either of his children would ever die before him. But when you live to ninety, that's always a risk—that the people you love die before you do. Sam had wondered so many times how his father could survive first losing his wife, the love of his life, and then his son. Sam started to wonder whether whatever happened in the war, even all those decades before, had created the type of man who could even withstand such deep, dark blows.

After Ben died, Sam realized there must have been more to Ben than the alcohol and drugs. That was just a mask for what likely was a mental illness of some type. When he was good, Ben was great. It was when he was bad that the trouble happened.

Sam had always wondered if his mom's death had been Ben's last nail in the coffin. He had always been very close to her. She was always worried about him. He felt protected by her. He was clean for a while. Things seemed to be going well for him. He had a steady job, kept an apartment. He was even starting to date again. But when she died, he fell back into his old ways. And then it was just a matter of time. She wasn't there to help him get back on his feet again. Sam wondered if Ben realized that when he took the drugs.

Maybe his brother had given up? Or maybe not. Sam didn't know. He didn't understand. He wasn't sure he wanted to. All he knew was that his brother was gone.

Chapter 56

ALTHOUGH SAM WAS anxious to get back to Nashville, his dad slept late. He didn't want to wake him since he knew how emotionally draining the trip had been. Sam needed to get back to work but convinced himself that another day would not really matter. Sam sat in the hotel room answering e-mails while his father slept.

By the time his dad woke up and showered, it was late morning, so they had brunch at the hotel. Then they packed up the car and headed back to Nashville.

It was a quiet drive, only about three hours. Sam realized that his dad was tired. Max slept most of the way home and hadn't eaten much for breakfast.

Sam was worried about the toll the trip had taken. It was a lot, both physically and emotionally. Sam focused on the road ahead but could not stop the thoughts that were buzzing around him. Some were about work, some about Lynn and the kids, and most were about what he had just experienced these last few days with his dad.

Sam started thinking about all the road trips his family had taken where his father had been the driver. It was how things were supposed to be. His dad was the leader of the troop. His mother deferred to her husband's place in the family's hierarchy. When Ben and Sam started picking on each other in the back seat, they expected to hear their father's serious but playful warning, "I will pull over. Don't make me come back there to separate the two of you!" They would dutifully comply until the roughhousing started again when one unintentionally brushed against the other. Sam remembered how his mother would turn around and smile, reassuring the boys that their father was only trying to keep them safe but still loved them.

As the thoughts swirled in his head, Sam recognized that he was distracted while driving. He glanced at the radio and increased the volume. The station was still set to the seventies. It startled him a bit that this song was playing. Sam loved the Beatles, John more than George. But "All Things Must Pass" by George Harrison had always haunted him.

"All things must pass. None of life's strings can last.
So I must be on my way and face another day.
All things must pass.
All things must pass away."

Sam reached for the radio and pressed another button. Any button. Those words were very real to him. They reminded him of his childhood anxieties and his thoughts about death. That he would live his life one day without his parents. It frightened him then, and it frightened him now. That feeling of impending loss would often engulf Sam when he lay in bed at night as a child. He loved his parents. He didn't want to grow old because he knew if he grew old, they would too. Sam honestly understood the reality that the loss is overwhelming no matter how old you are or how old your parents were when they died. No matter the age, it is still the loss of a parent, the only people in your life who love you unconditionally.

His eyes turned towards his father. The man was different than he remembered from when he was younger—smaller, weaker, and feeble. But he was still his father. It was clear to Sam that no matter what age his father was, he possessed a power that could never be extinguished. He was his father. The man who raised him and was always by his side. He was his protector.

Sam understood it was different now, but it didn't remove his fear of loss. He remembered how it felt when his mom died.

"All Things Must Pass" rang in Sam's ears.

They arrived back in Nashville at about four. Sam drove up his father's driveway and parked. His dad had fallen asleep again, and he gently shook him awake. He was able to help him to his room and stayed nearby as his father washed up.

They sat in the den watching the news as the afternoon dragged on. Little was spoken between them. When it got closer to dinner, Sam offered to run out and pick up something to eat, but his father told him that he wasn't hungry.

By 7:30, Max had decided he was going to bed.

"Long day, son," his father said. "Thanks again for driving. I'm hitting the sack." Sam watched as his father pushed himself out of his recliner and pushed his walker along the hallway down to his bedroom.

Sam said, "Goodnight, Dad." But he did not feel comfortable leaving his dad alone that night and added, "I might just crash here tonight, too."

"Whatever you want, son, whatever you want."

He switched the channel on the TV. He was tired himself. The trip had been draining. He texted Lynn his plan. She responded with an emoji heart.

Sam wasn't sure what triggered it, but his mind flashed back to when his parents had taken him and Ben to the beach as kids. It must have been somewhere in North Carolina, maybe Hilton Head, but all Sam remembered was their time playing, building sandcastles, trying to avoid the waves, and playing catch with a football. Sam realized what a cliché it must be to carry more happy memories than sad ones. He knew that his mind could only recall experiences of true joy or wretched sadness. Everything else seemed to be disintegrating photo albums in his brain, snapshots here or there of experiences, both with his family growing up or early times with Lynn. Then, there were more recent memories of Aaron and Lucy. But the fog was growing. Sixty years of life. So much had happened.

Sometimes he felt like he failed to appreciate his past fully and wondered if he had failed to pay attention. So much had happened. He wanted so much to remember it all, but he couldn't. He certainly understood now that less of his life stood ahead of him than behind him.

Lynn always seemed to have a more precise memory of people, events, and moments. She remembered the emotions of what had happened while Sam fought to remember those moments that seemed so much clearer for Lynn. Sam found himself trying to recall those memories, both the good and the bad. It was becoming harder for him.

He fell asleep on the couch with the TV still on. It had been a very long day.

When he woke up in the morning, Sam waited to check on his dad. He carefully turned the knob on his bedroom door to avoid the loud creak. He didn't want to awaken him if he was asleep. He took a few steps into his room. His dad was sleeping, snoring slightly. He seemed okay.

He decided to let him rest. He would leave a note. He stepped back out of the room. As he closed the bedroom door behind him, he looked back at his father. He had learned so much from him during this trip, but he chastised himself for waiting so long. Sam had spent so many years looking at this man as his father that he never really stopped to see him as a person. He was a man who had been through so much. He had his challenges, disappointments, and failures, but he never complained. He always wanted Sam and Ben to be happy. He never troubled them with his worries, anxieties, or fears. Sam just remembered some of the lectures, the "fatherly words." Sam realized those words were how his father communicated his concerns to his sons.

"Always be true to yourself."

"It's a long race, a marathon, not a sprint. No shortcuts. Plan for the long game."

The words stuck in Sam's head. He had tried to share those lessons with Aaron and Lucy too. As he walked back to the den to get his things, he understood that he actually had been listening to his father all those years.

Chapter 57

A FTER SHOWERING AND changing at home, Sam went back to his office. He had a lot to do to catch up. He was feeling the stress of the last few days.

When he saw Lynn that morning, he promised to fill her in on the trip when he got home that night. He was otherwise too rushed. She understood.

When he walked into his office, Sam collapsed into his chair behind his desk. He stared at his computer for a few long minutes before opening the dozens of e-mails he had refused to read while on his trip. It was an arduous process, especially since most of them were case related and contained attached documents that were the pending matter that Sam and his team were handling. It was exhausting, and Sam found himself an hour later, only having accomplished a portion of his review after having been interrupted to take a client call and answer a question from one of his associates. He knew he was still tired from the trip. The driving had not only been draining, but he realized how aware and attentive he had been the whole time in watching his dad, making sure he was doing okay.

The world didn't care about his time with his dad. The world had its own expectations about getting things done and never seemed to stop. Sam knew he would have to "pay for it" when he returned to the office, but he had not realized how much his perspective would change by being with his dad on this trip. Sam counseled himself to appreciate the time that he had spent with his dad. He knew that sometimes the expectation of everyday work life was too consuming for him. The recognition that life was fragile and all too short was openly present for him over the last few days. And it made him think.

He asked himself how he would spend the remaining days he had been given, whether he would live another day or until he was ninety? He realized on the trip that he had been on this earth for sixty years. He had spent the last thirty years working his ass off to support himself and his family. Would he spend the next thirty years doing the same? Sam shook his head at the thought of burning those years away working. He was aging too. His parents had both had a long run. He still couldn't get over that his dad was ninety. It was incredible.

He had battled with these questions of work and life before. He had already shifted his life when he moved his family to Nashville ten years earlier. Maybe it was a mid-life crisis, but it had turned out for the best. Now here he was, ten years later, challenging his assumptions for the next ten years. Should he continue to work? Should they downsize and start to travel? Had he saved enough for their retirement and to help Aaron and Lucy in their lives and maybe their grandchildren? Should he even impose such responsibilities on himself that way? Sam didn't have the answers to these questions as he saw more and more e-mails accumulate.

Sam knew in his heart, really understood, that after he died, any obituary published about him would simply tally his thirty or more years of his work into one sentence: "He was a lawyer." Sam recognized that what would take up the most space in his obituary was that he had a loving family. At the end of the day, he knew that the only important thing in his life was his family.

As he often did, Sam then mentally traveled to a place where he would not have any responsibilities. A place where he could simply enjoy being alive. He called it "retirement." Then the phone rang. It was as if he had woken from a hypnotized state. He shrugged off his daydream and grabbed the phone.

"Sam Silver," he said as he answered the call.

Chapter 58

S AM FELL BACK into his routine at home and work pretty quickly. Before he knew it, it was already Friday. The week had passed quickly.

Sam had stepped back into the case and dealt with the witness problems and other pre-trial issues. It had been an exhausting week. The trial was only two weeks away.

He was finishing his first cup of coffee when his cell phone rang. He didn't recognize the number and assumed it was a spam call, but he felt he should pick it up with everything going on. "Hello?" Sam said. More like a question than a greeting.

The voice was quivering. Out of breath. "Mr. Silver. It's Dorothy. I was working at your father's house this morning. He looked very bad. I called 911."

Sam was piecing it all together. It was Friday. Dorothy cleaned his dad's house on Fridays. So, it was the housekeeper calling. About his dad.

"911?" Sam questioned, still trying to get clarity in his head about the uncomfortable call.

"Is an ambulance there?" Sam asked quickly before she could respond.

"Yes, yes," the woman said. "The ambulance. They are taking him to the hospital."

"What hospital are they going to? Please ask them."

The voices sounded faint, muffled. "They are going to the

Veterans' Hospital. I hope it's okay that I called them. I was very scared."

"Yes," Sam said to reassure her. "Yes. Thank you. Please tell them that I will meet them at the hospital. Thank you." He repeated the instructions to her again. Then Sam hung up the phone. His heart was beating fast. There was fear in his mind, but the adrenaline pushed him forward. He had to get to the hospital. He grabbed his coat and looked back at the paper piles on his desk. It didn't matter. He had to leave. He would finish later.

Walking to the lobby, he tried to organize his thoughts. It had only been a few days since they had gotten home. Sam knew his dad was tired from the trip and had been weaker, but he didn't expect this emergency. He had been so busy that he had not taken the time to check in on his dad. Sam had moved on to the other spinning plates in his life. He had intended to stop by, but he hadn't. He had texted but not called.

Sam walked past the receptionist. "Tell Jack that I had to leave. I have to go to the hospital." As he got to his car, he called Lynn and told her what was happening. She said she would meet him at the hospital. With traffic, Sam got to the hospital in twenty minutes. Having come from home, Lynn was closer and was already in the waiting area when he arrived.

A nurse escorted them back into the emergency room. His father appeared to be asleep on the gurney. Sam could see that he was hooked up to various IVs and that they had monitors attached to his chest. "How is he?" Sam asked the attending nurse.

"He has been awake a few times, mostly when they were taking blood. Otherwise seems to be resting."

Another nurse came in a moment later and told Sam that they were watching his kidney and liver functions. They had given him sedatives to keep him calm and reduce ongoing pain. But the medicine made him groggy. It was the tradeoff for what likely would have been a situation where Max would have been agitated and maybe difficult to deal with. "We are hoping his levels get higher," she said.

Sam walked over to the side of the bed to look at his dad. His father's eyes seemed to be darting behind his eyelids. Sam wondered what he was thinking. He took his father's hand in his hand and squeezed. "I'm here, Dad," he said. He hoped for a response but accepted the peace of his father's sleep.

Sam and Lynn sat there for the next hour until the doctor came in to check on Max and update them with a report. They stood as the doctor entered the room.

"Nice to see you," Doctor Han said.

"I'm so glad you're here," Lynn said as she shook the doctor's hand. "My father-in-law really likes and trusts you."

It was reassuring for Sam to know that the doctor knew his father. "So, what happened? How is he?" he asked nervously.

"Seems like your dad is experiencing some liver failure. We're trying to manage that with some IV meds. The trick is to balance those meds with what he regularly needs for his heart and kidneys. We're worried we might see some shutdown if we can't get things to balance back in place. We'll know better over the next day or so how he reacts."

Sam had been listening but decided to interject. "He is scheduled to move to an independent living center in a few weeks. We have been packing up his house."

"Good," said the doctor. "It will be easier to provide the care he needs with 24-hour nursing services. But for now, we'll keep him in the hospital. We'll be moving him to a private room."

"Thank you," Sam and Lynn said in concert. As they talked, a nurse opened the curtain and pushed a cart into the area next to Sam's dad.

"She's just testing his potassium and iron levels," Dr. Han explained.

Max fidgeted when she took his arm. He opened his eyes.

"Dad. I'm here," Sam said.

His dad's eyes blinked and scanned the area in front of him.

"Ben?" he asked.

Sam stood there, unable to form the words to respond.

Before he could answer, his dad's eyes closed again.

"We need to keep him sedated a bit longer. Just to ensure he gets the rest he needs to let the medicine work. We'll try to draw him out of those by tomorrow," the nurse said.

Sam was focused on his dad. It had been a long time since he had called out for Ben. Sam was choked up.

He told Lynn to go home. He wanted to stay with his dad until they moved him into his room for the night. It would take another few hours. His dad would remain sedated. After his dad was settled into his room, the doctor convinced him to go home. "He'll sleep through the night," the doctor said. It will be better that you're here tomorrow when he is alert."

As Sam left the hospital, he couldn't escape his worry about his dad's poor condition. He worried that the trip had led to his exhaustion and dehydration and felt responsible. He tried to balance that against the reality that it was a trip his father wanted and actually what he needed to have. Sam understood that the trip may have still happened with or without him. Sam recognized the closure that his dad needed to return to the memories of his ship, the Bunker Hill, and visit Tony's grave.

He couldn't help but appreciate that his father had had the opportunity to experience the trip. He had left something on that ship that he had to get back. The trip was the other bookend of his father's life. He only hoped he had found what he needed. They were so much alike, both always needing to finish what he started. There was no in-between.

He was in his car when his phone buzzed. He looked at the number. It was Lucy.

"Lucy?" Sam answered. "Everything okay?"

"Hi, Dad. How's Grandpa?" She paused. "Mom called me."

"He's resting. The trip just took a lot out of him. He's dehydrated. He's getting fluids. He'll get his strength back."

"Okay. Well, tell Grandpa to get better," she said.

"I will. I love you."

"You too, Dad. Are you okay?"

"Yes. Just worried. You know me."

"Sure do. We'll talk later, okay?"

"Perfect. We will."

Lynn was already in bed when Sam got home. She had been reading and had fallen asleep. Her reading glasses were still in place, and the book was open. Sam hated to wake her, so he tried to be quiet as he undressed and washed up before he got into bed.

He was brushing his teeth when he heard her from the bedroom.

"Sam. How's your dad?"

"Sorry. Didn't mean to wake you," Sam said, walking back to the bedroom.

"I tried to stay up." She smiled. "How is he?"

"He's still out of it. I'm not sure what happened. He was pretty good on our trip. He seemed strong. He was with it."

"But maybe he used up his energy to make it through the trip. That was what he wanted. He wanted to go to the reunion, to say goodbye to his friends."

"But not to say goodbye to us," Sam responded quickly, feeling defensive.

"Get some sleep," Lynn said. "You can go see him in the morning."

Sam pulled the blankets aside and climbed into bed. He put his head on his pillow and stared at his ceiling before turning to his wife.

"I'm scared," he said.

"I know." She kissed him. "It will be all right."

Chapter 59

WHEN HE RETURNED to the hospital Saturday morning, his father was still unconscious. Sam was disappointed; he'd been hoping he'd be awake, alert, and okay. Instead, monitors beeped around him, his chest rising and falling as oxygen poured through his mask. He lay motionless. He was present but also somehow distant.

Lynn arrived a short time later. They spent the day at his bedside. There was little change. In the late afternoon, Dr. Han met them in Max's room and asked them to step out so they could talk.

"I'm sorry to tell you that it appears that your father suffered a stroke" the doctor said. "It's not uncommon based on the symptoms he was experiencing and his age," she added.

"When?" Lynn asked.

"We don't know. It could have been in his home or last night. The CT test confirmed it this afternoon."

So, what happens now?" Lynn asked as Sam was processing the report.

"I have to be honest," she said. "Based on our experience, it is doubtful that he will recover consciousness. And if he does, it is unlikely that he will have complete verbal or motor function."

The doctor waited for them to understand the severity of the information she had just provided to them.

"Anything you can do?" Sam asked.

"Your father is pretty strong willed," the doctor said, "but considering his age, there really is nothing we can do."

Lynn hugged her husband.

"I will want you to review these forms, including a DNR decision for you to consider," the doctor said as she handed them a pamphlet from the hospital.

"I'll let you review these and then we can talk later."

Sam told the doctor that he didn't want his dad to be alone and wanted to stay with him. The doctor reminded Sam that it "could be days" for his father.

"Yeah, I know," Sam said.

Sam and Lynn walked back into Max's room. They sat down the chairs next to his bed. Sam opened the pamphlet and saw the miscellaneous information documents about "palliative care" and the "Do Not Resuscitate" form.

As Sam understood from the doctor, even if his father gained consciousness again, he was unlikely to function independently.

Sam pulled up a chair next to his father's bed, Sam reflected on the night his mom had passed. The memories were vivid for him.

The phone had rung at two in the morning—a time when no call could be good.

As he reached for the phone next to his bed, he prayed it wasn't about Aaron. Lucy was home with them.

His voice was deep and crackling from sleep. "Hello?"

"Sam. There's an ambulance. They are taking your mom to the hospital. She's in a lot of pain."

Sam understood immediately.

"Dad. Are you going with them? Do you need me to come and get you?"

"No. I am going with them. They said I could, and your mom wants me with her. She keeps calling my name."

"Then we'll meet you at the hospital. It will be okay, Dad," Sam said. He knew the cancer was winning the battle despite five years of a courageous fight.

"She's a strong woman," his dad said. She's a strong woman," he repeated. Then he said, "I have to go."

The dial tone was loud in Sam's ear. He turned to Lynn, who was now awake and listening to Sam's conversation.

"They're on their way to the hospital."

"I'll get dressed," his wife said.

Sam had already pulled on pants from his closet.

It had taken only moments for them to exit their garage and head for the hospital. They decided not to wake Lucy, although they assumed she would have heard them talking or the garage door when they left. But if she were worried, she would call them. They could explain later.

At the hospital, they found their dad in the lobby. He explained that they had taken Rose back into an exam room and had asked him to wait for a report. He obviously had been in the way or otherwise was distracting to them. Now, he held his head in his hands. Lynn sat next to him and wrapped her arm around his shoulders. "She'll be okay, Max," she said softly.

"Let me check with the nurse," Sam said. He approached the nurse sitting in the triage area.

"Yes. They took your mother back to try to reduce her pain and give her fluids." Sam listened as the nurse read from her screen. "You'll be able to see her shortly. The doctor will come out to provide a report."

Sam thanked her and returned to explain the status to his father. "Dad, it may be a while. Do you want some coffee?"

"I'm fine," his dad said. "I'm fine."

Sam sat down on the other side of his father. Max was surrounded by love during one of his life's most difficult times. Sam had left messages for Ben but had heard nothing back. He didn't know of any other way to reach his brother. "Mom is in the hospital. Call me," was all he could say in his voice messages.

Moments later, the doctor told them she was resting and that they had given her the pain medication she needed. He explained that they would want to keep her in the hospital to manage her pain for a few days before they discharged her. She had already been moved to another room on the fifth floor where they could see her, but he recommended everyone go home and come back in the morning when she would be awake.

When they walked into her room, she looked to be resting comfortably. She did not seem agitated. They circled her bed, and his father took her hand and kissed her forehead. "Everything will be okay," he whispered to his wife. "We love you, Mom," was all Sam dared to say.

When Sam drove his father home that night, he assumed they would go back in the morning to see her. He was planning on staying with his dad at the house and returning to the hospital when visiting hours resumed. The hospital staff had given no indication that she was at risk. There had been many nights before, just like this, when she would have to stay over to get blood transfusions or additional pain medication. This night was just another awful experience, for her, but it didn't seem different.

But it was. The call came from the hospital at three in the morning. They called Max at home. A nurse from the floor told his dad that she had passed away only moments before.

She told Max that "her heart had given out."

Then Max had called Sam.

"She's gone" Max had told his son on the phone. "she's gone."

It would be a conversation and words that would remain with Sam forever.

Sam drove to his father's house to be with him. They sat together at the kitchen table. No words were spoken other than, "She's gone."

His father had lost the love of his life. He was in shock. Sam assumed that he had somehow prepared himself for this, but he had not. He had let his mind live in a place where she was going to recover, where her cancer didn't matter, and they would get past this. He had said they'd survived other battles and would survive this one. But now the reality was sinking in.

"Let's go see her," Max said as he rose from the chair.

Sam knew Lynn was on her way to the house to join them and would now go to the hospital with them. Sam had not heard back from Ben. He never got a chance to say goodbye.

Sam and Ben had rarely talked about their mother and what happened the night she died. Sam was uncomfortable with the fact that they had left her alone and hated how she had died without any of them there. But Ben had his own demons to deal with. He said his phone had died, and he'd never gotten Sam's messages. He blamed it on other people and other things. But Sam had gone to Ben's apartment the following day to find him. Ben was there, passed out, his apartment a shambles of empty liquor bottles, cigarettes, and daily lottery scratch tickets. The room smelled of mildew, smoke, body odor, and booze. But Sam wasn't surprised. This was how Ben lived. And Ben thought it was "all good."

When Ben's fog cleared with the news about his mother, he said something about how the doctors had messed up and that they should sue them.

Sam let him talk until the words stopped coming, and Ben sat quietly.

"Mom is gone. I can't believe it, but it's true," he said to his older brother. Sam was looking for something from him. He wasn't sure what. But it was a moment when Sam needed his older brother to comfort and care for him. They had just lost their mother. But it wasn't going to happen.

"I need a drink," Ben said. "Let's toast to Mom."

Sam just watched as his brother stumbled toward the kitchen to find a bottle of anything.

"Ben. Go take a shower and get dressed," he said. "I'm going to bring you over to Dad's. Lynn is there. Friends are starting to come over. You need to be there. I'll wait. But make it fast."

"Got it, little brother. Yes, sir." And Ben took the bottle, walked into the bathroom, and closed the door.

Chapter 60

SAM AND LYNN left the hospital to go home, have dinner, and shower. Sam didn't want to leave, but he needed a break. He would return in the morning. Lynn offered to cook something for dinner. Sam poured himself a bourbon and went outside to his back porch.

What bothered Sam the most was that he had waited so long to talk to his father about his early life. The man had a life before he became a father. His adventures and his struggles made up the person that became his father. Sam should have wanted or cared to know more. It was only now, at the end of his days, that he had expressed interest or concern. He had waited too late to discover who his father was. Sam thought, "Do we wait too long to learn about our parents? Who they are? What they did? What their lives were like? Do we take it all for granted until it's too late?"

Sam pondered the realization that we are all guilty of ignoring the inevitability of the finite nature of life. Our guided expectation of one hundred years is just a hopeful perspective against the reality that there is an ever-turning carnival wheel that stops regularly, and another player loses his turn. We see death all around us: in friends who lost their parents while still young, children who die by accident or addiction, and contemporaries suddenly felled by cancer or heart attack. It surrounds us. We grieve, we think, and then we move on.

Sam thought about his mom and his brother. Their lives, dreams, goals, joys, memories, expectations, solutions, creations, and interactions were over. They had lived their life on this earth.

They were no longer—what a loss. Sam cringed at someday losing his same connection. Lynn, Aaron, Lucy. They would all go on, but he would not be there to watch.

Sam shuddered at the thought of waking up every day and going to work as if that day could be wasted because there was always the "next" day. He thought about how most of us work each day while believing that our fun and joy can be sufficiently saved for weekends and holidays. He was troubled by the naïve assumption that life lasts forever and that there is always "another time" to do something. "The days go by fast," Sam heard himself say.

Sam thought about his father. He was ninety. Maybe that longevity was why Sam didn't usually worry about dying himself. He understood Ben's death to have been an accident, something Sam understood as an avoidable death. So, he rationalized that as long as he did not abuse his body with drugs and alcohol, Sam would be safe from that early fate.

Sam thought through all of the calculations about how he could live a long life, but he also realized that none of his plans or schemes would guarantee him or anyone else an extended life.

His recent test results from his doctor only heightened his recognition that we are made just of blood, cells, and organs and that sometimes, those parts fail. Whether we were made by God or science, we are somehow just flesh and bones and will not survive forever.

Sam got up from sitting on the lounge chair and went back inside.

When he got to the kitchen, he could see that Lynn was visibly upset.

She said "The chicken. It's too damn dry." She was crying.

Sam put his hands on his wife's shoulders. "Everything will be fine," he said.

He laughed. "With everything going on…..you're worried about the chicken?"

He kissed his wife. He held his kiss for an extra moment.

For Lynn, it was her husband's reassuring way of calming down a distraught wife who was internally trying to hold her family together.

For Sam, he was thinking about how lucky he was to have his wife by his side. With everything that had happened, Sam was anxiously and consciously aware of how fragile life had become. At that moment, he was worried that this kiss could somehow be their last. He did not want to take it for granted.

Chapter 61

S AM GOT TO the hospital early the following day. He had not slept well, expecting the call in the middle of the night, but the nurses said there had been no change.

He continued his reflections from the night before. Sam thought back to when he was a child and worried about the day that his parents would die. He had thought about it and cried about it when he was younger. He didn't want to live without them in his life. He couldn't imagine life without his parents.

It was these types of anxieties that kept Sam from being a "happy" person. Sam tried to be happy but recognized that part of what always overwhelmed him was measuring his life by some type of "happiness" scale. He knew that using such a scale overshadowed life's simple successes. He had a job and a family, and he fed and kept a roof over everyone's heads—but there was an inherent pressure of somehow being "happy" in life, whatever that meant.

It surprised and even impressed Sam when he met people who always seemed upbeat and happy. They didn't have to be rich or feign wealth to be happy. They just seemed to understand and recognize that life is short. You have to make the best of it, one way or another. They seemed to find joy in everyday living rather than succumbing to the pressure of "What's next?". Sam could not get past the fact that he was wired with the problem of "What's next?" He had worked in his profession for over three decades. Some would even say successfully. He had held his marriage together, had helped raise two wonderful kids, and cobbled together enough for his family to be safe, educated, and even travel the world. Yet, he was not satisfied. He craved something else, although he could never artfully express what that craving was.

Sam thought at times that he had partially resolved this absurd quest for happiness. He tried to explain to his kids that it was a simple farce, that there undoubtedly are moments of happiness and occasions of bliss. That there are undoubtedly slices of pure health, joy, and peace in our lives. But there is no status of happiness. It is a feeling, not a constant condition. It is in the ebb and flow of life that one measures true happiness, the recognition that with the good comes the bad. He wanted them to know that they should appreciate the moments of happiness that they have, rather than the constant quest for happiness.

Happiness was not a topic that Sam could easily share with his friends. Sam knew that everyone had their crosses to bear. It always felt inappropriate to discuss happiness with others when many were dealing with illnesses in their family, troubled children, or unemployment. Sam was seeking answers to these perceived woes from an audience with its own challenges. Sam used those circumstances to seek perspective on his troubles. But it didn't work.

Sam also did not talk to his parents about these thoughts. He didn't want them to worry. Over the years, Ben had gone through his series of jobs, struggled with his mental health, and fought through failed relationships. It was a lot for them to handle. They did not need to add Sam and his "happiness quest" to their list. Every time he stepped forward, his dad seemed to have enough on his plate. Ben. Work. His health. Then Mom got sick. Sam knew he would have to face his future challenges on his own.

As a father, he invited his kids to share everything with him. His nonjudgmental approach made him available for any questions or worry. But he soon realized, especially as they got older, that they were much like him. He was convinced they would rather internalize their issues than add worry to their parents' lives. He was sad about that. He wanted them to be different. But he began to assume that this was how life worked—the evolution of strength from the parents to the children. We care for them when they are babies so they can care for us as we age and need help—the circle of life.

Sam just wished that whatever he learned as he added on the years could somehow be shared with his kids so they would not suffer in the same way. He wanted to tell them that life is short; stop worrying so much. But it was impossible to explain that to children who see their lives as just beginning. "Let it go," Sam would remind himself.

He hoped that if there were ever a time that his kids needed him, they would understand unequivocally that nothing mattered more than they did to Sam. They could ask him anything, no matter what else was going on. That, to some extent, their existence was the driving force in Sam's life. The door was always open, no matter what.

What bothered Sam the most was that even though he wanted to communicate all of this "wisdom" to his kids, he struggled to find the words, or even the courage, to talk to them about it. Instead, he wondered: Was he overstepping, interfering, and somehow constricting their ability to grow and learn for themselves?

So here he was. All this time had passed. They were grown. They had their own lives. It was becoming tougher than ever to balance his goal of being their parent, advisor, and protector while now letting them manage their own lives. Ultimately, Sam wanted to connect with his children the way his father connected with him. His father never overstepped but was always there when Sam needed him. There was always an available ear. No judgment. Sam hoped he played the same role in his kids' lives.

It was about twelve when Lynn arrived. The partially opened door shifted as she came in. "Hi, honey." She kissed her husband on the cheek. "Any change?"

"Nothing. He's here, but he's not."

"I'm so sorry." She looked at her father-in-law. She had known the man for almost forty years. Then she stepped forward and tilted her head to whisper in his ear. "We're here, Max," she said softly, kissing him on the forehead. "We love you."

She had truly been a daughter to him. The daughter that he never had. Max used to tell her that if he'd had a daughter, he wished it would be "a girl like Lynn." She loved that. It was a special connection. She treated him differently than his sons did. Maybe it was just the difference between sons and daughters. His initial hesitation about her not being Jewish when Sam and Lynn married had melted away over the years, especially when they came back to Nashville.

Sam loved that this dad loved Lynn. Sam had always gotten a kick out of watching his dad with Lynn. He thought of he as a daughter and loved her as if she was his. It had been different with his mom and Lynn. They competed for Sam's attention, so their relationship had more challenges. His mom had been tough. But through it all, Lynn had remained the dutiful daughter-in-law, even though sometimes the meat had been "overcooked" or the kids were not dressed "warmly" enough for the weather. Over the years, his mom was forever trying to make Lynn Jewish. She got her wish when Lynn converted. And they were inseparable once Lynn moved back to Nashville to help her when she got sick.

Sam smiled.

"Why the smile?" His wife looked confused, especially considering the circumstances.

"He loves you," Sam said. Sam rose from the chair. He stepped toward his wife and gave her a long hug. "I'm going to miss him," he said gently to his wife. She pulled him closer.

As he held his wife, Sam determined that whatever he had to do to manage his own battles, he would. He would listen to his doctors. He would do what he needed to do. His father had taught him again about fighting the battles you face. His father had learned his lessons young. It had taken time for Sam to truly understand the fight. He knew he had a lot of life left to live. "Thank you," he said.

"The kids know." Lynn said. "Anyone else we should call?" she asked.

Sam thought for a minute. He had one cousin from his dad's side of the family, but they were not close. She lived in California. They had not seen each other in decades. It was Jacob's only daughter.

Sam thought about his uncle Jacob, his dad's only brother. He had passed away already over ten years earlier. He had retired and moved to Scottsdale for the warm weather. His father had stayed in touch with his brother, but they also were not very close. Sam recalled that after the war they had both returned to Brooklyn. Although older than his dad, Jacob had gotten married later in life, had the one child and then divorced. He remembered his dad saying that Jacob had suffered from "battle stress" or what was now called "PTSD". Sam wondered if his father had experienced something similar from his experience on the Bunker Hill.

Sam responded "No. It's just us. We're his family."

Chapter 62

SAM WAS ANXIOUS. He hated hospitals. It had been four days. Max was still fighting.

While he waited, Sam couldn't help but think again of his own mortality, considering his recent test results. Sam hadn't had time to wallow in his internal pity about his possible cancer. He wanted to rise above that, to be stronger. He knew that after this situation with his dad was over, there would be time. Another week or so would not change his prognosis. Even with the subtle fear surrounding him, he was convinced he would be fine. He had learned more about handling adversity in the last two weeks than he had ever understood before.

It was inevitable that Sam went through the "What ifs?" running through his brain. Had he done enough to ensure Lynn would be okay if he weren't around? What about the kids? Would they be okay if he wasn't around anymore? Had he earned sufficient savings? Did he have the right insurance?

He almost tortured himself—but life was life. He had done his best. Plus, he was sure he would be okay, that whatever treatment he decided on would work. But his heart sank when he thought he might not be around to walk Lucy down the aisle at her wedding or that he would not get to meet his future grandchildren.

He had to stop thinking like that. He would be fine. Sure, he knew that there were no guarantees in life. He could be hit by a bus tomorrow without any advanced notice. That was how things worked. Sam realized that worrying about his plans for the future would be a wasted effort. "God laughs," Sam said to himself. It was odd, he thought, to be so worried about this: After all, his mother had lived until her mid-eighties, and his dad was still around. He had "good genes," people would say. He just wanted to ensure that Lynn and the kids knew how he felt about them. But they did. He was sure of it. Things had not been left unsaid.

Sam waited with his dad. And as he waited, he couldn't help thinking this time with his dad was proof that life is short, even at ninety. Things came to an end, and he had to get his priorities right. He had to. Even if he had cancer, Sam knew this would not be the last battle he would fight.

Chapter 63

I T WAS ALREADY Wednesday, and Sam had been sitting there for almost the entire day. He felt himself nodding off as the hours passed. Lynn had been with him in the morning, and friends had stopped by to pay their respects and support Sam. There was a community of friends that Sam and Lynn had developed over the last ten years. Some had known Sam since he was born. He would not leave the hospital. He didn't want his father to be alone like his mother.

Sam shifted in his seat. The vinyl chair with the wooden arms gave him little comfort as the hours had become days. The faux leather materials almost squeaked as he adjusted himself to get comfortable. He checked his phone for messages. Nothing new. It had only been just a few minutes. Time seemed to be a bit endless.

There was a soft knock, and the door opened to the room once again. Sam didn't initially turn around since he assumed it was another nurse or friend visiting.

"Dad?" the voice offered.

Sam turned in a rush. He knew that voice. Sam rose to see his son. He stumbled a bit as he reached for him. Sam extended his arms for a long overdue hug.

"Sorry I wasn't here earlier." Aaron was taller than Sam. His taut black t-shirt showed his size and strength.

Sam stood on his toes to fully embrace his oldest child.

"How?" he asked.

"Mom," Aaron said.

Sam smiled. He pulled back from his son and held him by the shoulders. "Thank you for being here," he said. His eyes were moist from the bittersweet joy of the moment. He turned back to his father lying in bed, the monitors beeping as the oxygen pumped through the mask. "Grandpa knows that you're here," he said.

Aaron moved closer to the hospital bed and cradled his grandfather's hand in his own. "Hey, Grandpa," Aaron said. "I'm here." "Sorry, Dad," Aaron added as he noticed the quiet pain in his father's expression. "How are you holding up?"

Sam smiled. "Much better now. Really. I feel like I have so much to tell you."

Sam stood there next to his son and his father. He looked at his son. "It's really good to see you."

They both stood there for a minute to get their bearings. Then Sam pulled a chair against the wall forward so they could both sit by the bed.

"What are they saying?" Aaron asked.

"It's just a matter of time," Sam replied. "He had a stroke. He's not coming back."

"Can he hear us? Does he know we're here?"

"I think so. I really do." Sam knew that it didn't matter. Being there was more for Sam: to be with his father at the end.

"How was the reunion?" asked Aaron.

"It was really meaningful. Some stories about the war that I never knew. He lived through a remarkable experience."

"I never knew," Aaron said. "Will you tell me?"

"He has a great story." Sam found himself smiling. "Plus, some life advice that you'll just love to hear, too."

"I thought you two had the same playbook."

Sam felt a rush of joy from those words. "Yeah, same book. But your grandfather had much more practice time on the field."

"I can't wait." Aaron said it in a funny, sarcastic tone, but Sam knew he really wanted to talk.

"You know, I worry about you" Sam said to his son.

Aaron hesitated. He was looking down at the ground. He simply said, "I know." Then he added "I don't want you to."

"How's life?" Sam asked, moving closer.

"Busy. Always busy. But doing okay" he said to his father. "I seem to be better able to balance it all these days. I have good friends. It all seems to work."

Sam felt relieved to hear this from his son.

"Sorry for our regular guilt trip," Sam answered. "I know that we reach out a lot. It's just that we don't see you anymore. Don't seem to hear from you."

"I know. I'm sorry." Aaron paused to find the words. "I just sometimes get caught up with everything. I should be better. I miss all of you."

Sam reached his hand over to his son's arm and squeezed. "We know. We miss you too." He paused. "As long as you know we love you and support you."

"Always," his son said. "I know."

The two men sat next to each other. It had been too long, but they had just reconnected. A gap in each of their lives had been filled.

"And I'm seeing someone," Aaron said.

"Really? Great!" his father replied.

"Yeah, and get this: She's Jewish!" Aaron said with a sly smile.

"Miracle of miracles," Sam said, smiling. "Wait, tell your grandfather. This might be the news he needs to finally wake up!" Both were laughing. "Remember your bar mitzvah?" Sam asked his son. "Your grandfather dancing during the hora?" Sam smiled again. "I had never seen him dance before. Boy, he was happy. His only grandson. That was something." Sam turned to look at his own father. "Remember that, Dad?"

Aaron watched his father talking to his father. His joy was replaced by the sadness of the moment.

Sam turned back to his son. "Can I tell your mother... about the girl?" Then he smiled. "Better yet, you should. She'd love to hear all about it."

"Okay, Okay." Aaron said.

Sam looked at his father. His breathing was shallow, assisted by the machine. "I don't know if you knew this about your grandfather," he said, "but he almost died in the war. There were back-to-back kamikaze hits on his ship off of Okinawa. Two planes, two bombs. It was a miracle that he lived. There were over four hundred men killed or missing and over two hundred wounded." Sam repeated what he had heard and read about that fateful attack. "It was only days after the war in Europe ended, and just three months before the end of the war in the Pacific. The last great battle of World War II. He received a purple heart."

Sam continued his story. "This trip. It was so he could say goodbye to his friends. We even visited one of his shipmates at Arlington Cemetery—the man who saved his life."

"Wow," said Aaron. "It must have been emotional for him. I never knew about the war."

"Exactly," Sam said. "It was part of his life. Part of who he was. He never tried to make it part of our life. It would have been too much. Too sad." Sam hesitated, then added, "It made him a better father and grandfather."

The two sat there reminiscing about Max and some of his exploits. It seemed odd that they laughed out loud as the oxygen pumped life into the man beside them, but the stories made them feel more connected with Max and each other. A few times, Sam had to control his laughter in front of the nurses who came to check on his father.

"I'm going to stay here for a while. Why don't you head home? Mom would love to see you," he said to his son.

"Okay. I need a shower. We'll have dinner later?" Aaron asked.

"Sure," Sam said as he rose. But he knew he would not leave the hospital until it was over. He did not want his dad to be alone like his mother when she passed. He wanted to be there for his dad, just like his dad had always been there for him.

Again, Aaron reached for his grandfather's hand. As their hands met, Aaron whispered his goodbyes.

Sam held back tears.

Then father and son hugged again. "Grandpa would be happy to know he brought us back together." Sam kissed his son's cheek. "All we want for you is to be happy. No expectations, no demands. Make the best life that you can. If you can find someone you love who loves you back, there's nothing like it."

As Aaron left, Sam returned to his father's bedside. He took his hand. There was little warmth. He squeezed it gently. There was no response. "Did you see that? Aaron's home," Sam told his dad. Sam understood that his father had tried to teach his children resilience and fortitude and had tried to show them what it meant to have faith. Most importantly, he had shown them what it meant to love. Sam vowed as he sat there to ensure he did the same for Aaron and Lucy if he hadn't already. His dad's life would have that legacy, along with more.

Now, more than anything, he wanted to share Max's lessons with Lucy and Aaron. He had to. His responsibility as their parent was to share this knowledge, this wisdom. They were still just starting their lives. Things had been easy up till this point. He and Lynn had seen to that. They had bandaged every skinned knee. Sam thought of his children as strong and independent. They weren't unprepared, but life was tough and unpredictable. There were always rainy days.

Aaron had already turned thirty. Sam had been thinking a lot about what his life had been like when he was thirty. He had been in the early years of his law practice, just getting started, but already feeling the pressure of the world as he balanced family, work, and life.

Sam enjoyed the coincidence that his dad had been thirty when Sam was born and Sam was thirty when Aaron was born. When his dad turned ninety, it was a unique circumstance that the ages were ninety, sixty, and thirty.

Sam wanted to somehow give Aaron the playbook of how life was supposed to be handled. He thought that by helping his son, he could show him the shortcuts to make it easier. But he realized that whatever he had experienced was for him. His own life would not be a roadmap for Aaron. Sam's job was to try to be there for him, as his dad had done for him. Not to live his life for his son but to be there just in case.

Sam thought about what it meant to be a parent. It was all about offering unconditional love. To support your children but letting them live their own lives. Sam's parents had let him leave and go to New York. It all had worked out for the best. And now Sam would have to let Aaron and Lucy live their own lives. He and Lynn had prepared them as best as they could. No matter how much Sam worried if they would be okay, he knew they would be.

But life can be very hard. Hopefully, some joys outweighed the challenges, but he knew that each of them would face those challenges, and Sam could do nothing to stop them—just as his parents could not control what had happened to Ben.

Sam always wondered what his dad thought about Ben. He rarely spoke about it. If he felt regret, shame, or heartache, he didn't express it. For Max, it was just another of life's battles. But this battle to save Ben, his father had lost. Sam didn't want Aaron to make the same mistakes Ben had made. He was clear that, if nothing else, he would try to keep him from going down the wrong road. But that was all he could do. Life would take care of the rest.

Chapter 64

I T WAS THURSDAY morning. Sam's cell phone rang. He answered the phone even though he did not recognize the number.

"Hello?' Sam said.

"Hello" was the reply. "This is Rabbi Litman from Temple Shalom."

Sam realized it was the rabbi from his dad's synagogue, he was asking to visit with his father. Sam said "of course".

When he arrived, they chatted for a few moments about what had happened.

Rabbi Litman was a relatively new rabbi at the synagogue. The congregation's Senior Rabbi had retired a few years ago. Sam had not yet met this new young rabbi.

As he spoke with him, Sam felt like that rabbi understood that his father only had a short amount of time left.

The rabbi pulled up one of the chairs in the room to sit next to Max's bed. He reached for a prayer book that he had brought and leaned closer to his father. Sam watched as he spoke quietly to his father, the words soothing and sweet, like a parent to a child. Then he turned to Sam. "Sam, it is customary to offer a confessional prayer. Do you mind?"

"Please. Thank you."

"The prayer is called the 'Vidui,'" he said, taking Max's hand. "It's a chance to express our regrets and our hopes. It is spoken before our soul departs from the body."

The rabbi recited the prayer and then spoke further to Max in hushed tones. Sam just watched the tender exchange and felt strengthened by the experience of the tradition he was grateful to be witnessing.

The rabbi began to chant. Sam heard the Hebrew verse, almost like a song. The sound echoed in the small room. Sam was moved by the experience. Sam knew that his father would find meaning in the prayer.

When he was done, the rabbi rose and stepped forward to speak to Sam.

"I've been fortunate to have spent some time with your father. He attended some of our senior events in the past year."

Sam was happy to hear that.

"He was always a pleasant man. Thoughtful. Sincere. He really was a mensch."

"Thank you, Rabbi, thank you," was all that Sam could express at the moment.

"If you need anything, just call me. When it is time, we will help you with the funeral."

Sam stood and shook hands with the Rabbi. He held his hand for an additional moment, considering a possible request for him to help Sam find his faith again. He didn't know how to put it into words, but he wanted to talk about his challenges with his beliefs. He wanted to discuss how he had given up on God when his mother and brother died and how he longed to find his faith again. But Sam resisted. It was not the right time. Maybe they would discuss it later.

"Thank you again Rabbi" was all that Sam could say again. He looked into the rabbi's eyes for connection.

When the rabbi left the room, Sam sat and spoke to his father.

"That was nice dad." Sam said to his father. The rabbi seems like a good guy."

As he spoke, Sam felt a positive strength for his father that at the end of his life, he still had a connection with his faith and that the rabbi had been there for him. Sam wondered for a moment again about his own life. He accepted the fact that he had not really lived a Jewish life. He couldn't recall the last time he had even been to their synagogue. He thought it probably had been when Lynn did her conversion.

Sam understood that being Jewish was part of who his father was, it was part of his identity. Sam had internally acknowledged many times that he had chosen a different path. But Sam knew that these recent days would make him re-examine his beliefs. He knew that he would try to start on the path again toward reconnecting with his Judaism. He knew he would honor his father by being open to his religion and his heritage, by being open to finding a possible connection to God once again. He had to start by accepting what had happened in the past with his mother and brother and thinking about the future.

Sam laughed to himself. Even Aaron was dating a Jewish girl. "That must be a sign" Sam said to himself.

As he watched his elderly father, Sam was glad his mother was not alive to see her husband suffer. She was too pure of spirit. Sam thought that it would have been more than she would have been able to handle.

Sam had time to think as the hours continued to pass. Maybe too much time. His head was buzzing with thoughts about life and his dad.

He had thought he would still have more time with his dad. But his dad knew better. That was what that conversation had been at the bar that night: a way to prepare Sam for when the time came. He was planning on going over to the house on Sunday. Bagels and corned beef. But now, that visit wouldn't happen—not ever again. Something so innocent and routine would disappear, just like his dad. One day he was there; the next, he wouldn't be.

It was then that Sam heard the monitors change their sounds. Softer beeps grew a bit louder. The rhythm of the beeps became faster. It was subtle, but Sam knew it was different. Sam watched as the stiffness of his dad's shoulders appeared to soften, and, with his eyes still closed, Max's head seemed to turn in the direction of his son. "Dad," he said, startled.

As he had experienced so many times before, Max's subconscious was reliving those moments when the explosion had blinded him in a cloud of darkness, and the vibration of the bulkhead steel had stifled his hearing after the bomb's detonation. His mind raced again to the prospect of death by suffocation as he searched for light or air. And once again, as in life and his repeating dreams, he found an escape as his aching and bloodied body moved toward the open hatch. Again, he felt the pain of burning skin as he climbed the scalding metal rungs of the ladder toward his freedom. He was climbing toward freedom.

Sam watched his father lift his right hand. His eyes were still closed. Sam leaned over his dad's hospital bed and grabbed his father's hand. "I'm here, Dad. I'm here. You're safe. You made it out. You can let go."

And Max let go.

Sam felt his father's hand soften within his own. He knew he had held his father's hand for the last time. The sound of the monitors changed to a monotonous tone, and the nurse entered the room. She checked Max's wrist for a pulse. "I'm sorry, Mr. Silver," she said as she began to turn off the monitors connected to her father. Sam stood there for a moment that felt like a lifetime as she removed his mask and the wires connected to his chest.

When she finished, his dad lay peacefully in the bed as if asleep. Sam imagined him now with his mom. Sam knew that he would be back with them and Ben one day. He was a 60-year-old man, but at this moment, he felt like a young child. He had just lost his father, his best friend. He leaned over and kissed him on his forehead. "I'll miss you, Dad." Then he backed away, unsure of what to do next. The room felt cold, quiet.

Sam's eyes moistened. The tears came quickly and easily. He didn't remember crying at Ben's funeral. He was so angry about Ben's death that he never let it get to him emotionally. And now here he was, the last one in his family. Everyone who'd known him as a child was gone. He felt immediately alone. Like his childhood had never really happened.

Sam once again, contemplated what death meant. After losing his mother and brother, it seemed like death surrounded him. He had started to read about it. He read books by secular and religious authors that explored the meaning and purpose of life. Rather than ignoring the inevitable, Sam began to prepare for it. It became part of Sam's reality that life was finite. He thought he was smarter and more aware of this than his friends and co-workers. He didn't understand how they could be so oblivious to the simple reality that time on earth was limited.

Sam tried to be rational about all of this, but it was sometimes just too hard to think about the end of life. He wasn't sure that he was even supposed to contemplate it, the ultimate disappearance of one's spirit in the world. He clearly understood that it was hard to fathom the fate that awaited him and everyone around him, but he wanted to understand it so that he could push himself to live a better life while he could. Sam often found himself at work saying to himself, "What am I waiting for? Life is short," but then he would go back to work and ignore his own admonition. Now he took a deep breath and accepted that everyone approached the concept of fate differently. "Dust in the wind." Sam thought about the words, again hearing the song in his head.

Because of his mother and brother, Sam already understood the sadness and pain of being the one left behind when someone dies. He felt like he knew it all too well.

This time, Sam turned his thoughts toward his father. Did his father have regrets? Was he at peace? Instead of sadness, Sam imagined something more pleasurable for his dad, like the release of his spirit from his failing body and his soul being reunited with his life partner, Rose. He tried to imagine them together. Now they would be together forever.

Chapter 65

SAM STOOD OUTSIDE his father's room for more than twenty minutes, trying to gather himself. He hadn't yet called Lynn. He knew she would be upset, especially since she had wanted to stay. She had been there all day as Max's breathing had faltered. But the doctors didn't know whether it would be two hours or two days, and finally, she had listened to Sam and left.

It wasn't long before one of the hospital administrators approached and offered her condolences.

"What happens next?" Sam asked.

"The funeral home is on its way. They will be in touch. You need to make whatever arrangements you want with them."

"Yes. That's right." Sam said. The quiet shock of the news was now slowly creeping into his brain. He thought of the funeral home. Picking the casket. Visiting with the rabbi. "Thank you," he said. But he didn't know what else to say.

Sam would stay with his dad until the funeral home came to recover him. Sam waited outside the room when they moved the body onto the gurney and covered him. They explained that he would be cared for under Jewish tradition, which included a ceremonial washing and wrapping of the body, and that someone would be with him at all times until the funeral.

Sam thanked them and waited until they left the hospital. Then he called Lynn. She had been waiting. She told him she knew when she left that it "wouldn't be long." She listened to Sam ramble about the last few moments of his dad's life and responded, "I love you, honey."

She then just told him to come home and that she would call the synagogue. "Don't worry," she said. "They have done this before— and I'll tell the kids. You can talk to them later. Just come home".

Sam walked somewhat aimlessly to his car. For a long moment, he sat inside motionless, trying to organize the rapid and repeating thoughts in his mind. He thought about a funeral. He realized the burial plot had already been long paid for when his mom and dad picked their spots at the local cemetery. Even the tombstone was already in place since his dad had selected a double monument inscribed for both of them when his wife died.

As he pressed the button to start the car, music rang from the speaker. It was still set to the Frank Sinatra station that his dad had picked for their drive home. Now, "My Way" echoed through the car. Sam shook his head and smiled; this had been one of his dad's favorite songs, and somehow, hearing it made Sam feel better. "The power of belief," Sam thought to himself. Maybe his dad was still out there somewhere.

Chapter 66

THE FUNERAL, IN accordance with the Jewish faith, was held as soon as the body could be buried, so long as it was not Shabbat. They decided that the funeral would be held on Sunday. It was a beautiful day. Late May in Nashville had that impending summer warmth in the air combined with the remnants of spring. Clouds hid the sun, and a subtle light bathed the mourners surrounding Sam and his family, who now stood in front of his father's casket. It was a simple pine wood box adorned with a wooden star of David. "Ashes to ashes, dust to dust," the rabbi had said.

The casket was laid across a metal scaffold that would lower the box next to his wife, who'd been buried there just a few years before. They would be together again. It was what Max had wanted, talked about and prepared himself for: an eternity to rest in peace next to the woman he had loved from the day he had first seen her.

Sam looked at the double monument that carried his mother's name and would soon include his father's, too. Their last name, "SILVER," was carved into the stone at the top in bold capital letters. The marble piece had remained incomplete for five years while his father waited to join her next to their oldest son. Sam stared at Ben's tombstone. "Son, brother, and friend" were the only words other than his name and the dates of his birth and death.

Sam could not help but flash back to the same setting just a few years before when his dad had been a mourner for his mother and then his brother. Now all that was left was Sam and his family.

The cars began to arrive, and the crowd started to increase and surround the tented area where the burial plot had been excavated and the coffin had been placed. Under the tent were the seats for the immediate family, older relatives, and friends who wanted to avoid direct sunlight. It was going to be a sunny day. Not especially hot since it was only the middle of springtime, but the humidity started to climb as the morning dew began to disappear. The funeral had been set for eleven, and the rabbi would begin on time. Sam understood. His father's funeral was just one of the number of funerals he might handle that day, that weekend, and that week. Max may have been one of the oldest in the group. Less of a tragedy when you think about it compared to others who died younger, like Ben.

The rabbi interrupted the gathering to announce, "We'd like to get started." Then he spoke into the microphone attached to a small metal podium. "Let's all gather together now. If you are joining us in the tent, please take your seats."

Sam, Lynn, Aaron and Lucy sat in the front row. Then others who chose to sit made their way forward and sat in one of the folding chairs that had been placed in the small tent. Others who were attending encircled them, rows deep. As the service began, two sailors, dressed in formal dress uniforms, unfurled the American flag that they would then rest over his father's casket. As they finished, they saluted the casket as they would any high-ranking officer.

The rabbi then welcomed the community and expressed his condolences to the Silver family. He explained to those attending that he had the pleasure of knowing Max personally, describing him as a son, brother, father, and grandfather who was loved and admired. Furthermore, the rabbi explained that Max wore the "crown of a good name," a tribute far more valuable than a person's wealth. The words soothed and comforted Sam, who felt that the rabbi was speaking from his heart. Sam focused either on the rabbi or the casket, which stood only a few feet away. It seemed impossible that his dad was actually in the coffin. His father had been a part of his everyday life for so many years now that Sam shuddered to understand what his life would be like without him. He'd had a clear purpose in life when he returned to Nashville to be with his parents, and that was even truer after his mom passed and his dad became a fixture in his daily life.

A moment later, the rabbi began to musically recite a prayer for the living, and Sam reached up to his collar to touch the black ribbon that the rabbi had attached to his suit jacket. The ribbon was a substitute for the act of tearing one's clothes when a loved one dies. As if a part of the mourner's body had been torn away.

Then Sam turned to look at his wife, Lucy, and Aaron. They were a family again. His dad had brought them together.

After the Rabbi finished, he called Sam up as the next speaker. Sam rose and turned to the group that had assembled. So many familiar faces. Their family, friends, work colleagues, and friends of Lucy's and Aaron's that Sam had watched grow up with them. Many had been with them not that long ago for his mother's funeral. He considered himself a comfortable public speaker, but he knew these words would be difficult, if not impossible, to present without a script. So, he had simply written a letter to his dad for all to share.

Sam unfolded the white sheet of paper that he took from the inside pocket of his suit jacket. He hesitated, knowing that he had poorly cobbled some words together before going to bed the night before. He was certain that the words would not do his dad justice. How could you eulogize a man of ninety years who had lived a full life, built a family, a home, and a career? He had touched so many lives. Sam just thought about what a strong man his father had been. And then this week, being at the reunion with his walker. What an odd realization about life and the years of toil a body can handle.

He began, "Dear Dad." As he spoke, he looked at the casket and the striking colors of the American flag that draped it. The eulogy lasted only a few minutes. Sam tried to hold back his tears. He thanked his father for being his rock and safety net. "I knew you were always there to hold me up or to catch me if I fell. I'm glad I came home to be with you and Mom. I know you thought you were a burden to us at the end, but the truth was always that I needed you more than you needed me."

When Sam finished, Lynn, Aaron, and Lucy surrounded him,

and there was a group hug. Lynn kissed her husband and grabbed his hand as they all returned to their seats.

A short moment later, the rabbi called up Aaron and Lucy. They were Max's only grandchildren. They gathered hand-in-hand behind the temporary lectern and microphone. Lucy unfolded the single white sheet where she had written her notes. Her voice quivered as she looked at her father. Then she began to read. "I wasn't happy about moving to Nashville when I was fifteen," she began. "I had my friends in New York, our old house, a neighborhood I knew. I didn't understand why we'd moved. But shortly after we arrived, I went for a long walk with my grandfather. I wasn't in the mood to listen back then. I was sure my parents had been wrong about moving. That they had destroyed my life. But Grandpa explained what it meant to him to have our family here. That it would forever change his and my grandmother's lives that we were back. He told me that I had to understand what being part of a family meant. I know that I didn't understand what he meant back then, but I have come to over the years. I could always go to Grandpa when I wanted to talk about something, if I needed something, even if I fought with my parents. He was always there for me. And after my grandmother died, I knew he was so happy that we were there for him. Sometimes, I felt I was given a special gift to have my grandfather in my life. He was always so supportive of us. I'll never forget his kindness, his smile. His hugs." She stepped back to give space to Aaron.

"He wanted to be my fraternity brother," Aaron began. The gathering laughed. A sense of relief permeated the room. "Not that he was the 'Bad Grandpa' like the movies, but he always wanted to hear the stories when I was in college. He'd rib me about my girlfriends, and he always had a beer in the fridge for when I came back to visit. It's not like he lived vicariously, but he wanted to hear about school, work, and everything I was doing. He was always telling Lucy and me how proud he was, but he always wanted us to be careful. "Stay out of trouble,' he'd tell us. I don't know how to say this, but when you think about the devil on one shoulder and the angel on the other, he was my angel. I admit there were times when

I thought, 'What would grandpa say about this?'" Aaron smiled and then gathered his composure. "Thanks, Grandpa. I still have you on my shoulder. I'll be careful, don't worry."

Lynn grasped Sam's hand with her own. These were things the kids had never said to them about his dad. At that moment, all the anxiety about moving back to Nashville dissipated. It was okay. They were okay. In fact, they may even be better for it.

As they returned to their chairs, Aaron and Lucy circled their father. He took both of his kids in his arms. He squeezed them tight. "He loved the two of you. You know that, right?"

Both said, "Yes."

"And you know I love each of you, right?" Sam moved his gaze back and forth between his two grown children. In his mind's eye, Aaron was still seven, Lucy only three. It was still difficult to see them as adults. Sam didn't accept that he was sixty either. Life had moved way too fast.

"Dad. It will be okay," his daughter said. She always said the right things.

Sam accepted that they didn't realize how vulnerable their father was. The last gauntlet of old age had stepped aside. Sam was now the oldest. The mantle of seniority was now Sam's to bear. He didn't like it one bit.

As they settled back into their seats, the rabbi began to chant some final prayers before asking the family to rise to recite the Mourner's Kaddish. As Sam recited the words, he heard the friends who had come together reciting with him. Although the prayer seemed haunting when read, Sam knew it translated into blessings to God with an appreciation for the life we have been granted.

At that point, the same naval honor guard approached the coffin. As "Taps" played, they removed and folded the flag his father had fought for seventy years earlier. An officer approached Sam with a folded American flag. "Courtesy of the United States government," the sailor said to Sam. Sam rose, and the man, in full honor uniform with white gloves, handed him the flag. "On behalf of a grateful nation," he said. Sam accepted the folded flag and looked again at his family. It was only then that Sam accepted that his dad was back on his ship after seventy years. He had escaped death then but now had rejoined his fellow crewmembers lost that day. Sam thought about what his father had told him about Tony.

The final portion of the funeral included the opportunity for the family and others in attendance to "make a soft bed of earth" for Max by filling the burial plot with soil. Sam watched as the rabbi demonstrated the tradition by scooping three shovelfuls of dirt, the first with the shovel facing down to demonstrate your reluctance for the act of burial, but the remaining with the shovel up to complete the task. The sound of the dirt landing on the lowered casket echoed in Sam's ears and was difficult to hear. He finished his turn and handed the shovel to Lynn. It was a somber act, but Sam understood it was considered a mitzvah to care for your loved ones, even to the end.

Sam was greeted with hugs from friends, co-workers, neighbors, and community members. The sun had broken through the clouds, and the beams of light brilliantly cast their rays into the cemetery. He turned back toward his father's burial plot and watched as the light bounced off the marble tombstone, highlighting their name as if in bright lights.

Sam closed his eyes. He saw images of his mother and father watching him and his brother as children playing in the backyard of their house. It was a happy time, but a long time ago.

Chapter 67

THE HOUSE WAS eerily silent. Sam could not remember when he had been in the place without his dad there as well. He sat at the kitchen table and half expected his father to shout from his study or walk into the kitchen to make some coffee. But it was quiet. Sam could hear the air conditioner rumble in the basement, and the drapes waved back and forth as the air blew from the vents in the floorboards.

Sam stood up and walked into the living room. He glanced at the framed family pictures that sat above the fireplace. All of them were old and yellowing. The largest was a family photo of the four of them. The picture had been taken just after Ben had started high school at some family event they had all attended. They looked happy. At peace. A static moment of existence when life was so much simpler. He stepped closer to look at the faces of his parents. What did they expect of their lives? What did they fear? It all seemed so innocent. How was it that they could all leave him? Sam felt alone. Here was an image of his family at a perfect time, but it was now a faint memory. It was just him now.

He closed his eyes. Flashes of memories of his family when Sam was younger passed through his mind. It was just yesterday. But now, here he was by himself. He felt sadness at a loss, not just of his family, but of time.

He walked into his dad's study. The cardboard boxes from his effort to pack for the move were scattered around the room, filled with his dad's trophies and commendations. A life filled with achievement and appreciation, all now removed from the walls and placed in boxes. Sam stood frozen at the recognition that, at the end of the day, none of these things really mattered. They were things. It made him think of his own walls in his office at work. He had tried to emulate his dad. "I've worked so hard to achieve what?" Sam asked himself.

Sam scanned his father's desk. It was clean. All the stacks of papers had been removed. But in the middle of the desk lay a single large envelope. It was his dad's stationery. He reached for the envelope, which was thick and weighty, hesitating for a moment before pulling a letter out. He sat down in the worn leather chair behind his father's desk. The handwriting was hard to decipher, but clearly his father's.

As he read, tears welled up in Sam's eyes.

"Dear Sam:

Thank you for taking me to Washington. It was a special trip for me and hopefully for you too.

I lived a good life. That's all you can ask for. I had over sixty years with your mother by my side and the blessings of two wonderful children. I tried not to create expectations for you and Ben, but maybe I did. I hope they were not too burdensome.

Of course, your mother and I doubted ourselves for years about Ben and his struggles. But we also worried about you. You were equally important to us, and I hope you knew that. You made your mother so happy when you came home. We loved that you were an everyday part of our lives. I hope we contributed to your joy in life as much as you contributed to ours. Thank you and Lynn for everything you did for us.

Have no doubt that we knew how much you loved us. I know that you struggled to let us know that sometimes, but we did. Don't worry about that.

We loved you and your brother so much, sometimes so much that it hurt. It is the joy and the curse of being a parent. But don't take love for granted. Make sure you show your love for Lucy and Aaron. They are your only responsibility now. And one day, may you experience the joy of grandchildren as we did.

Hold tight to Lynn. She always reminded me of your mom. You were lucky to have found each other.

Find peace, my son. Life is short. Live happily.
Dad"

Sam was overwhelmed. His father had certainly just written the letter since they had returned from the reunion. Sam wondered if his father had known what was coming. He thought about what his father had told him in the bar about "being ready."

Sam pulled from the envelope the remaining contents.

Out spilled his dad's war medals. What stood out first was the Purple Heart. Then Sam saw his father's medals for participating in the Pacific and American campaigns from the War. Sam lifted each and studied its craftmanship. They were heavy in his hands. For more than 70 years, his father had kept them, but he had never really displayed or boasted about them. They were relics of his history. Sam held them tight as if he were holding onto a part of his father.

Also in the envelope was a second letter.

"To the men of the U.S.S. Bunker Hill:

I will always be proud of the men I served with on the Bunker Hill and glad to be considered one of them. I will never forget the men who died that day to save our ship. They had the spirit that gave us our land and our liberties. Although the experience of this misfortune of war is long over, the pride in how these men sacrificed themselves will never be forgotten. The story of the Bunker Hill will remain as immortal as will her dead heroes."

Sam sat back in his father's chair, looking up to the sky. Sam smiled as he let his feelings sink in. Sam held the medals in his hands, trying to think of the right words. Finally, he took a deep breath and leaned further back in the chair.

As he looked upward, Sam simply said, "Dad. I love you."